The Time of Long Shadows

Jeff Neilsen

ISBN-13: 978-1-7322105-0-9

Malitok

For Andrew

Let me tell you a story...

Table of Contents

Foreword

The inspiration for this book comes from my youth. The work of none other than Edgar Rice Burroughs took me to places outside of even my television-addled imagination. Adventure in Africa, on Mars, and Venus; in strange places like Pellucidar, at the center of the Earth, and the island of Caspak wove their way into the wonderful body of knowledge I received as a result of the reading. Month after month, year after year, in truly devout bibliomania, I followed Lord Greystoke, John Carter, and all the other heroes. The lessons learned were too numerous to count, so full were the stories, as much with human frailty as with strength. I think perhaps the most important thing I learned from the books was that in all situations that humans might find themselves, courage is possible.

One strong piece of advice for young readers: If you find a word you do not know, look it up.

The Time of Long Shadows

Introduction

This story takes place on Malitok, the single large continent that occupies nearly the entire surface of the world known as Aarden. A look into the evening sky reveals three moons. You, the reader, are not at home. The civilization is pre-industrial–but just. The population of Aarden has been changing at a phenomenal rate, and in an unusual manner. Ultimately the course of this evolution will be discovered. This story focuses on Gorrenn, a young man who lives in farm country. His life, and the lives of everyone in this world, are about to undergo many extraordinary changes.

1

Listen close, or listen not at all, I will come to thee,

no less than other men.

- The Song of Death

Gorrenn climbed the path toward the top of the hill with purpose in his strides. He felt the need to put as much distance between himself and what was behind him as possible. When he reached the top, he continued on without a single glance back. What was back there would soon be only a memory, and a mental scar or two. It was the Time of Long Shadows. It was the time of year when each day the sun hung farther south in the sky. The land was cool at night, and each night would be colder than the last. He had to make speed to the next village, perhaps a real town. As well as he could with his heavy pack, he walked swiftly along the road.

The road provided easy going for a foot traveler, but left a single man exposed to all threats, seen and unseen. While he walked, Gorrenn kept his eyes and ears tuned to all his surroundings. He knew that there were many ways to fall prey in this world. He knew that many animals, and men too, could bring his journey, and his life to a halt. The wind, rustling the scattered leaves about, masked sounds that Gorrenn would otherwise easily pick up. This was a problem. Gorrenn knew he had to work harder to be more vigilant because of it.

The town he was leaving behind was called Daffin, a farming hamlet on the Broad Plain near the middle of Central West, largest of the Accord of States. It was just a cluster of eleven simple houses belonging to the farmers who worked the lands around the village. There was a modest store, adjoining one of the little houses. Lastly, there was a humble worship hall. It was all the small group of farmers could manage.

Daffin was where Gorrenn had grown to manhood, or what he understood as his manhood anyway. Fifteen Summers: He counted from the time he was taught his age, measured by the sun's passing its highest point in the sky each year. At the age of fifteen, Gorrenn was well in his seniority as a man. Few ever lived past fifty years of age.

One of the houses, in the small village, was his home. It belonged to Assh and Borrda, the people who raised him. Now, he was leaving it, never to come back.

That was what the people of Daffin wanted. That was the way it had to be.

Gorrenn was brought to Daffin as an infant by his father. Assh and Borrda were known to be childless. Unknown to him, Gorrenn's father had provided a considerable boon of coins to Assh and Borrda, so that they would not refuse when asked to raise and care for Gorrenn. At first, they were unsure that they should accept such responsibility. They recognized the scars and marks on Gorrenn's father as signs of his being a Fighter and Warrior. The thought of having such a child was daunting, to say the least. Fighters and Warriors did not live alongside other men.

In the end, Borrda's heart had yearned so intensely to have a child for such a long time that the choice was made. They took the babe-in-arms, and the boon of coins with calm determination. The agreement was set with the customary wine and bread-breaking: Assh and Borrda would raise Gorrenn as their own, telling him of his father only at the time of his coming to full manhood.

Like all the people of Daffin, Assh and Borrda were farmers. Their farm was larger than the others surrounding the village, but not the largest. The grain crop they grew every year made bread for them, and provided some to trade for necessities at the store. The feed-fowl, and hogs made for the meat, to eat and trade as well.

Borrda insisted on keeping her own vegetable garden, "No need for all the extra trade." was what she said, but she really enjoyed the work of tending the garden. Assh had taught Gorrenn the work of farming, and husbanding the animals. Borrda had taught Gorrenn the intricacies of the vegetable garden, and to read.

Few of the things he learned from Assh and Borrda pleased Gorrenn as much as reading. He quickly surpassed

Borrda's abilities and began to seek out books from other families in the village. In the books, he learned of the World. He read about the single, enormous continent of Malitok, with its Great Plain, the mountain ranges in every part of the continent, the lakes region, the coasts of the immense ocean sea. He read of wind-ships that went forth on the ocean, to islands far away, many weeks and months by ship travel.

Gorrenn read of the Traditions, the way of connecting the people to the days, weeks, months, and the years. Season by season, the Traditions kept the people in a rhythm with the world itself. He learned the Malitokan calendar. The weeks were comprised of nine days, each reflecting one of the Traditions. A month was seven weeks, again each reflecting a Tradition in itself. Each of the four seasons contained two of the eight months of the year. Year Day, the first day of each year was set aside from any of the months, and helped to keep the calendar in synchrony with the sun's march across the heavens.

For Gorrenn, reading was a form of transportation unlike any other. Without moving his body, the words, and drawings in the books he could get in the village, would take him to other parts of the world. Able to sit for hours at a time, he could read, and reread passages to get the most meaning and sense out of them. The books in Assh and Borrda's house came to be page-worn over the years of Gorrenn's repeated examination. If a new book were to be brought to the little village, Gorrenn would be sure to hear of it. His enjoyment of reading was well known to everyone in the village.

***

Like so many of the villages on the Great Plain, Daffin had a store to supply the families with necessities they could not generate for themselves. Haggs was the keeper of the Daffin's tiny store. He worked a small plot of land behind his homestead growing vegetables, and like everyone else, grain. His wife, Ligga, and their twelve-Summer daughter, Tornnel, worked alongside him to keep the farm up. They managed to have the store open at times the village people needed. Since their home was adjoining the store, in the village center, they contributed much to the collective effort to maintain the worship hall.

Haggs was a man that most folks would call small. He was shorter than most men by about a head. Nature had compensated Haggs for this by providing him with attractive features, and an earnest, honest personality. His mate in life, Ligga, was the taller of the two, and unlike her husband, not particularly attractive. Again, to offset this shortcoming, Ligga had the sweetest disposition of anyone in the village. Warm and inviting to all who stopped by their little store and home, many villagers went to the store for nothing more than to have Ligga remind them of beauty in the world which rewards the heart. Another gift at her disposal – one that offset her sweet manner perfectly – was her voice. Calm and soothing to the ear, it played upon your sense of hearing like a fine lute.

Gifts are passed from parent to child. So it was with Haggs' and Ligga's daughter. Tornnel was blessed to have both the sweet temperament and dulcet voice of her mother, along with truly an appealing appearance. Many families in the village looked to the time when Tornnel would be interested in a husband. Many believed that her twelve Summers had only begun to reveal the extent of her beauty.

2

Greet me warmly, in the fullness of your days, or

flee from me with all your might, I will embrace you, no

less than other men.

- The Song of Death

The largest of the eleven farms surrounding the village of Daffin belonged to Laeffas and Tremilla. Larger by more than half, the farm often required hired hands brought in from other villages. Even though most of the villages in Central West were operated solely by the farmers who lived on them, men came from the cities and towns, seeking simple work, even if it was only meagerly paid. Laeffas' and Tremilla's house was largest of the eleven in Daffin, but noticeably so only to the other farmers.

Laeffas and Tremilla themselves were people whose physical dimensions exceeded the norm. Both were tall and heavily built. "Stocky" was the word used to describe them, in kindness. When Laeffas and Tremilla lapsed into attempting to lord over the other villagers by virtue of having more farm than the others, less complimentary words were used to characterize them. The village of Daffin existed only in a sense of communal effort for protection from depredation by natural forces, as well as man-made forces. When group decisions needed to be made, no one had any more sway in determining the course the community would take than any other.

Laeffas' and Tremilla's son was Prodiggan. There simply was no better word than "Oaf" to describe him. Gifted as he was with even more of his parents' enormous proportions, he had few redeeming qualities. He was easily half again as big as any of the men in Daffin, with exception of his father, Laeffas. And, even considering his enormity, he was overweight. He was too fond of eating for the amount of activity he got.

His main focus in daily life seemed to be letting as many people as he could know that since he, his family and their farm were all big, that he was entitled to a significant amount of respect and, no less, reverence. Chief among his many frustrations was that few people paid him any mind, much less respect, at all.

Prodiggan went to some great lengths to make sure that the men hired by his father knew that he was someday going to be in charge of the farm. The hirelings managed to take in all in stride, just something else they were paid to put up with as menial workers. Most of the men who were subjected to this ongoing harangue thought of Prodiggan's coming of age as a good time to move on to other work.

As difficult as they might be to get along with in most regards, nature had not forgotten to bestow upon Laeffas and Tremilla gifts of their own. Both had been born with singing voices that were truly remarkable. Indeed, their singing had brought them together in the first place. In their mutual fourteenth Summer they had traveled to the town of Ahngrist, a commercial center for the center region of Central West. Each had come from their respective small villages to perform in the annual Third Harvest Festival singing competition.

First, Laeffas had sung a mighty oratorio from a popular opera, receiving thunderous applause from the gathered crowd. When his performance was followed by an absolutely stunning performance of an operatic aria by Tremilla, the crowd at first was silent. Then slowly the audience members began to clap and cheer even more uproariously than they had for Laeffas. The competition judges were at a loss as to which of the two was better. After some very lengthy consultation with one another, it was decided that they should both be awarded the Grand Prize together. All the members of the audience and competitors agreed that the decision was perfect!

Laeffas and Tremilla decided that Tremilla would take the Grand Prize trophy home, and that Laeffas would come to retrieve it for the second half of their wining year. As you might expect, being somewhat similar in general proportions, and gifted as they were with similar talent, nature took hold of the situation, and some months into the year after they had won their award, they were pledged to be married.

Prodiggan himself was, of course, blessed with vocal talents. It surprised no one when he began singing, even before he could walk. Babbling the most unintelligible nonsense in a voice that occasionally did coax the birds down out of the trees, Laeffas' and Tremilla's son bore all of the combined talent of his parents. Learning to speak, for him, was just a protracted singing lesson.

So, here was a most unique little family: Parents who could sing their respective hearts out, joined by a son whose vocal talents were unbounded. Laeffas and Tremilla farmed in the most earnest fashion, and lived in a world of music and merriment. The metaphorical fly in the ointment was that in his thirteenth Summer, Prodiggan was disinterested in pursuing any development of his considerable singing ability. No amount of coaxing, persuasion, or cajolery would bring him around to the intentions of his parents. Laeffas and Tremilla both had shared their visions of Prodiggan signing in cities such as Acquain, or perhaps even in Malitoka, First City of the Accord of States. Prodiggan wanted no part of it.

This friction being a matter between the family members, it was kept 'indoors', and not discussed outside the family. As a result of this, no one else in the village new of strife between Prodiggan and his parents. The young man knew what his parents wanted for him, and in the typical way of youth, he resisted the idea. Sullen and downcast, Prodiggan went about his chores, and what little learning his parents could provide for him with an apathy that set the whole family on edge. It was this very edginess that led to Gorrenn being sent away from the village of Daffin.

3

Care not too much for your life, it is balanced to

naught on my scales.

- The Song of Death

The little village of Daffin was home to another family, Stansso, Wildda, and Jolangg. Stansso was a farmer, like all other people in the village. His contribution to the communal life of the tiny hamlet was leading the worship on First Day, each week. He was the kellar of the small community. When the little congregation came together, Stansso would recite the Nine Traditions, citing the generally accepted meaning of each one, and elaborating on the specific Tradition for each of the eight months of the year. The First Tradition was reserved for Year Day, the one day of the year not part of any of the eight months. Originally accumulated as oral history over the millennia, The Nine Traditions gave a point of focus for the communal life of the people. Since each of the eight months of the year was sixty-three days long, each Tradition bore long discussion, thought and meditation. Each of the nine days of the week was also dedicated to a Tradition, with First Day always being dedicated to Life. The other eight Traditions, Grace, Truth, Fairness, Giving, Belonging and Family, Sharing, Work and Learning, and Death, all stood their place in the march of days, and the flow of one month into another.

Stansso's wife, Wildda, kept the house closest to the worship hall, and managed to stay ahead of keeping the hall clean and tidy. Their house did not adjoin the worship hall. This was a minor tradition in itself, an arrangement that grew out of respect for the importance of the Traditions. Even though the same plot of land held both buildings, they stood separately, as a sign that The Traditions were *for* men, not part of any man.

Stansso and Wildda had a son, Jolangg. Since neither of his parents were very big people, he was slight of build, and a bit shorter than average for his age. Like his parents Jolangg was very involved in learning the Traditions, and would someday carry on his father's work of leading worship, and teaching the Traditions. Born at nearly the same time that Gorrenn came to Daffin, the two boys had been friends since their earliest memories. Learning to read under the alternating tutelage of Borrda, and Wildda, they grew not only to know the Traditions

19

well, but each other. Gorrenn recognized early on that Jolangg's desire to study the Traditions was much greater than his, but did not feel any slighter for it.

Another family in the village was Stefirro, Drimmbia, and their fourteen-Summer daughter, Llakani. Tall, dark haired, and fair-skinned, Llakani was, like her mother, beautiful. She was one Summer younger than Gorrenn and Jolangg, and friendship grew among the three beginning at an early age. The three of them were nearly inseparable. When work on the farms, learning, and travel gave way to free time they were nearly always to be found together, usually in some playful enterprise or another.

Over the last year or so, the friendship between Llakani, and Gorrenn had become more of a focus for each of them than for the trio. Gorrenn at first noticed that Llakani looked at him differently than at Jolangg. She had begun to spend more of her time speaking to and eliciting responses specifically from Gorrenn. Jolangg was never left out of conversations, he had simply had his place in the trio shifted ever so subtly. The time shared together was always for the three of them, but Llakani and Gorrenn were beginning to get more out of it than they had anticipated.

Stefirro was the community's traveler. His farm kept drayage horses. When the village could send grain to the merchant town of Ahngrist, his horses would do the pulling of the wagons. The grains that grew on the Broad Plain were able to render crops several times a year, and trips were made to sell the grain, and buy supplies for the village as needed. Drimmbia often accompanied Stefirro on these journeys, often at the reins of her own wagon. Llakani, had been allowed to travel with her father and mother since her seventh Summer.

4

Wear the cloak of family and friends warmly, I

will take it from you.

- The Song of Death

Continuing to walk along the road, Gorrenn reached
into his pack for a small clay jug that Borrda had filled with
water. Allowing a passing sense of regret for having to
leave his mother behind, he drank from the jug and
replaced it in his pack. He thought of the fact that Borrda

wasn't his mother after all, and how he had come to learn this so recently. It would be enough water for today, but no more. He would have to watch for other sources of clean water along his path.

Gorrenn knew that the road he was on led to Ahngrist, where Stefirro sold the grain and bought supplies for the village. He remembered the town from trips he had taken with Assh when he was younger. He had also learned much from listening to Stefirro, Drimmbia, and Llakani report on their trips to members of the village who inquired of them. Gorrenn was only interested to learn what was reported and never made inquiries of his own. He had not thought it ever likely that he would need any more knowledge about Ahngrist than what he learned from listening.

Gorrenn did not know how long the journey would take on foot. The dray horses made the wagon trip in a day, but he had never considered the likelihood of walking any great distance. What he knew about comparing men to horses was what you learned on a farm. A man could outrun a horse, but only for a short distance. A man could walk all day and night, but a horse needed rest after half a day of riding or pulling a wagon. A man needed to start his day with food. Horses were fed only a small amount in the morning, so the digestion wasn't interfered with. A horse usually received in larger meal in the evening, after the work of the day had been done. Gorrenn felt that these differences made horses somehow wiser than men, in a way he had no words for.

The light of the Long Shadow day began to lessen. The day had been cool, but not cold. He always liked Long Shadow season, the time of year when Summer ended and the world began to cool before The Cold. It was the time of Third Harvest, usually a time of the best celebrations of the year. If people in other villages and towns celebrated at

Third Harvest, he did not know, he had never asked. He now realized that there were many things that he had not asked.

He didn't know how far he had come, or how much distance remained between himself and Ahngrist. Stopping by a tree that hung its branches low into a stream at the roadside, he refilled his water jug and decided to stay for the night. Gorrenn had slept out under the stars many times, but never this far from home, or his family. He hoped it would not be any different this night. He took a small parcel of bread from his pack and ate it along with a bit of cheese. Borrda had wept as she packed the food parcels for Gorrenn, he thought he could still feel the dampness of it on the wrapping.

He thought it safer, and wiser to spread his bedroll on the side of the tree away from the road, and where he might be able to see anyone approaching from either direction. How he had come to have an inclination toward needing safety was a mystery to him, he just needed to do things in this way.

Crickets and frogs began to chirp and sing, just as they did back home. This felt good to Gorrenn, and he began to relax, and settle in for the night. The three moons had risen earlier in the day, following their unique journey across the sky, always clustered together. Some called them the Three Sisters. Why this was, Gorrenn had never sought to learn.

Asleep, deep in the night, Gorrenn was awakened by what he at first thought was thunder. Then, he discovered that the sound he heard was hoof beats, fast approaching. Pulling his meager belongings close into him, he slid low to the stream bank to remain as far from anyone's sight as possible. The sound grew louder, the horse – and rider that Gorrenn could see silhouetted against the moons-lit sky – passed very quickly.

Gorrenn could not imagine that a man would have a reason to risk so much by riding at break-neck speed through the countryside at night. The danger of losing sight of the road, and reining the horse into a gully was great. Why would someone need to go so fast? Was it some great need, or some great fear that drove him on like that? Questions began to spin in Gorrenn's head. He shook them off, and tried to go back to sleep. The frogs and crickets had long since quieted for the night, and the gurgling sound of the stream was all that remained. It was enough lull him back to a fitful sleep.

When he awoke, Gorrenn realized he had slept later than he ever had on the farm. The sun was already well up above the horizon. Time for the first chores of the day, back home. A pang of regret and longing came to Gorrenn, and made him feel something he never had before:

weakness. As he ate from his small pack of bread and

cheese, he wondered why he experienced all these feelings.

He had no answer, other than to fill his water jug, pack his

bedroll, and continue his journey.

5

Take from others, flee to the farthest land,

I will ravage all you have gained,

and make it as nothing to you.

-The Song of Death

Two days earlier, just on First Day, was when

Gorrenn's life began to change dramatically. All he had

known before that day was the life of the farm, the work,

the land, the turn of the seasons, the four Harvest Festivals every year. Now he suspected he would learn much more than what the farm could teach him.

It was the First Day of the fourth week in Derrant, the first month of Long Shadow, the third season of the year. Worship had gone well, and the communal meal after was no different from any other. The balance of the day would be free time for all the people of the village to do as they wanted. Most would find ways to rest a little, a few would use the opportunity to work. The children and young people would play.

Since the ages of the children of the village varied widely, play involved games that were loosely structured at best. Toys and balls for sport were scarce, so many never-tried-before games came into existence. Most would fade from memory even before the end of day. As you would expect, a great deal of running about, chasing one another comprised the chief activity of almost all of the games played together on First Day.

At some time near the mid-afternoon, on this particular First Day, one of the chasing games began to get out of hand. Prodiggan had been nominated as the one to be sought. He would be chased by the other children. Even though he couldn't outrun even the youngest of the children, he enjoyed playing along, so he acquiesced, and was given a head start.

It did not take long for several of the other children to catch up with Prodiggan, who was so much larger than everyone else. Prodiggan was on edge, since his parents had not ceased to try and persuade him to follow his talent in singing. He was very unhappy that he had been caught so quickly by the other children, and lashed out at them, calling them all the rudest things he could think of. It didn't take long for a pack mentality to overcome the usual calm of the afternoon, and Prodiggan was soon surrounded by a group of taunting smaller children.

Gorrenn, Jolangg, and Llakani had not been participating in the game, keeping to themselves the way fast friends sometimes do, sharing commentary, and conventions of youthful wisdom between them. The three friends became curious at the sound of the game abruptly changing from the usual calls and laughter into jeering and shouting. Together, they trotted over to the play group to see what was the matter. The trio arrived just as Prodiggan raised his hand to strike Tornnel, who had allowed herself to stand too close, after delivering a particularly sharp invective.

"Don't!" Llakani screamed and lunged at Prodiggan, reaching out with her hand to intercept the blow aimed at Tornnel.

Prodiggan's hand struck Llakani's arm. The force of the blow spun her completely around, toppling both she and Tornnel to the ground. Prodiggan strode forward and stood over Llakani, his face dark with anger.

"You better get away!" Prodiggan bellowed at her. As he said this, Llakani started to get to her feet, stumbled a bit on the uneven ground and fell towards Prodiggan, pushing her hands into his ample stomach. This apparent insult made Prodiggan even madder, and he raised his fist, preparing to strike Llakani hard.

Jolangg, and Gorrenn had been just a step behind Llakani in getting to the scene of the upset, and watched in abject surprise as Prodiggan made to strike Llakani. It was just at this moment that Gorrenn's life began to change so very dramatically.

Almost without realizing that he was doing it, Gorrenn crossed the distance remaining between himself

33

and Llakani, in an instant. He began to sort Prodiggan out, completely. Gorrenn didn't know what he was going to do next, but he did know that he was going to protect his friend, Llakani from harm.

Even before Prodiggan could react to Gorrenn's sudden approach, Gorrenn grabbed Prodiggan's raised arm and twisted it behind him. As daunted surprise set in, Prodiggan found himself thrown to the ground. He then became the recipient of the most vicious blows he could imagine.

Confusion, fear, and anger drove Prodiggan to struggle to his feet and lash out with his other hand at his assailant, Gorrenn. Unthinking, and with lightning fast reflexes, Gorrenn dodged the blow, and drove a foot into Prodiggan's stomach. The force of the kick was enough to knock the wind out of Prodiggan, and he dropped to his knees, stunned and beginning to gasp for air. Gorrenn finished the confrontation by delivering a knock-out punch to the side of Prodiggan's enormous head.

The fight had drawn the attention of the rest of the children, who began to gather around the fallen Prodiggan. The violence of the confrontation had been intense. The aftermath of Prodiggan laying on the ground was too much for one of the younger children, who screamed. The scream attracted the attention of Drimmbia and Wildda, who had been deep in conversation, watching the children play from a distance. They arrived quickly. Wildda began to tend to the unconscious Prodiggan. Drimmbia soothed the younger children. Some of the older children ran to their homes, a sense of alarm guiding their instincts.

The scream also had the effect of bringing Gorrenn back, more or less, to his senses. Breathing hard, he stepped away from the fallen Prodiggan. He was unsure how it was that he had done what he had. It was confusing. He had not been angry, he had just acted. He was becoming aware that his hands now hurt from having struck Prodiggan a hard as he had. A sensation he had never felt before had overcome him while confronting Prodiggan. It was a sensation that was very hard to describe. It had made him feel like steel, and fire, and lightning all at the same time. Fading away now, the sensation was now a faint, susurrant buzz in the center of his head.

The experience of being almost overwhelmed by the new sensation, dispatching the lout almost out of hand, and now the fading sensation left Gorrenn drained, and confused. He was unsure what to do next. He was unsure what would happen. He sat down on the grass to try and figure out answers to these new questions.

Nothing of this sort had ever occurred in the tiny village before. While Gorrenn was still struggling with his own experience, Prodiggan's parents, Laeffas and Tremilla came running up to the scene of the fight, followed by Assh and Borrda. In short order, the entire population of the village was on hand.

Even though Prodiggan was quickly roused, his parents cast hateful glares at Gorrenn as they led him away to their homestead. Assh and Borrda, both with stricken looks in their eyes, walked with Gorrenn back home. When they arrived, Borrda asked Gorrenn to sit in the kitchen, while she and Assh spoke in their bedroom. Gorrenn did not know why there was a need for secrecy, it had never been needed before.

After a short time, Assh came in from the bedroom. "We'll speak tomorrow." was all that he said.

The little family ate their evening meal in silence. They spent an uncomfortable, largely silent evening waiting for the last light of day to fade. Late in the evening, Laeffas, Stefirro, Haggs, and Stansso had all come to speak with Assh. They spoke for a long time. Several times during the conversation, Gorrenn could hear Laeffas' strident voice raised, making an important point. Borrda had stayed at the house, while the men spoke at the edge of one of the fields. They all went to uneasy beds that night.

In the morning, Gorrenn awoke to the usual bang and clatter of Borrda preparing breakfast for the family. After washing, he asked Assh what work they would do that day, anticipating no surprises from the routine of farm work.

Assh simply said, "After we eat, we'll decide what's next."

Gorrenn was not used to answers that were not answers, but mysteries. Still, he sat down to eat, noticing that Borrda's face was flushed. She ate little of the food she had set to the table. Gorrenn was confused by all the unusual behavior around him, and ate only lightly as well.

After the meal, Borrda rose to clear the table. Gorrenn stood, intending to help as usual, but Assh put a hand on his arm and said, "We have to talk, now. Sit."

Gorrenn was glad that now he would learn what was the cause of all the upset, in their family and in the village. Assh began, "You came to us as an infant. You are not ours."

Gorrenn was stunned. The words seemed to slap him in the face. He did not want to hear them, but could not make them be unsaid.

"Your father brought you here, to us, just after you were born. He said he had been looking for a family to take you, because he could not care for you."

Gorrenn swallowed a catch in his throat and asked, "Why? Why couldn't he care for me?"

Assh looked at the floor and replied, "We never learned more than that your mother had died, and that your father could not keep you."

Gorrenn was filled with an uneasy feeling that seemed to replace all of his other emotions with emptiness. Borrda sat down, took Gorrenn's hand and said, "We had no children, in ten years of our marriage, and thought we had received a special gift when your father brought you to us."

The rest of the conversation seemed like a dream to Gorrenn. It seemed like a bad dream, one he could not run from, or even turn away from. With difficulty, Assh told Gorrenn of the promise they had made to Gorrenn's father: To tell him of his father when he reached manhood. Assh, and Borrda, both with much hand wringing, and tears on Borrda's part, told Gorrenn that they had decided that he was their son and would not learn of his father.

With their deception revealed, his parents went on to explain that the only thing they were sure of about Gorrenn's father was that he was a Fighter and Warrior. They had seen the scars and the troop marks upon him when he first appeared at their door those many years ago. Common knowledge of the ways of Fighters and Warriors was that they received troop marks when they excelled in fighting skills enough to be accepted into a cadre of Warriors. Each cadre had its unique way of designating their troop members, some with tattoos, some with branding. Marks were always on the faces of Warriors so no one would mistake them. Gorrenn's father had had both kinds of marks, unusual in the extreme.

Also, in the common knowledge of Fighters and Warriors, was that they live separate from other people. The ways of the Fighters and Warriors were so stridently violent that no other people could live with them, even near them. Their villages were very different from villages occupied by farmers. They had a strict code of honor.

The most important thing that all of the people of the Accord of States knew was why there were Fighters and Warriors in the first place. They fought on the borderlands against the Giants. No one spoke of the Giants. Like all children learning the world that they live in, Gorrenn had learned the rudimentary facts about how men existed in this world, not only populated with many wonderful beasts and animals, but with the unspeakable terror of the Giants.

Where the Giants lived, men could not. The Accord of States was established to provide protection for the lands where men lived. As men were able to protect more land, so the Accord of States grew larger, until now, when it covered the eastern half the continent of Malitok. The Great Plain of Malitok was where men grew their foods, raised their animals, built their villages and towns. Now, the

Accord of States encompassed lands in the hills on every boundary of the Plain. The Accord of States did not extend to the western half of Malitok.

Daffin was a village near the center of the center-most state in the Accord and that meant that the borderlands were far, far away. It would take days, even weeks to ride in a wagon to the borderlands. It could take entire seasons to make the same journey on foot.

When Assh and Borrda's words ran out, Gorrenn felt as though he had been whipped, not physically, but inside, in his heart. He sat for a long time not thinking, trying not to feel what he was feeling.

After a long silence, Assh said the words that stung worst of all, "You have to go."

6

Give all you have, or hoard it beyond the reach of

others,

I will spend your life, and waste your riches.

-The Song of Death

The midday sun was hot today, but it was already

nearing the midpoint of the season. Gorrenn thought that

perhaps it meant that a swing to much cooler weather could

be coming. He had seen the weather in Long Shadow

change dramatically, even in the few years he had witnessed it. The frosts of Long Shadow sometimes came quickly and without much warning. Even those with an acute sense of weather acumen were often caught off guard by the suddenness of Long Shadow frosts. Everyone learned to take them seriously.

In his haste to leave after Assh's revelations, Gorrenn had nearly forgotten his coat. Borrda had reminded him to take it, one last loving admonition as she stood crying in the doorway of their home. It was the only thing he presently had that could stave off even the mildest frost. It had been his blanket as he slept at the roadside last night. It was wrapped in a roll, around the perimeter of his pack, the way he had been taught by Assh, who told him it was the way the Fighters and Warriors did it.

Cresting a small hill, Gorrenn thought he could see the faint stain of smoke in the air just above the horizon.

The distance between him and any settlement was still considerable. He estimated that it would take another day's walk to reach as far as where the smoke rose. If the smoke arose from Ahngrist, the first part of his new life could begin.

Gorrenn had no idea what work he would be able to do in a town. He was not afraid of work. Work never seemed to tire him the way it did other men. Work, eat, and rest, and you were ready for another day. Seeing other men grow progressively tired as weeks and months of farm work wore on was a mystery to Gorrenn. This did not happen to him. In his years on the farm, Assh had always been the one to halt a day's work, whether for the midday meal, or for the evening.

The part of the Plain he was now crossing had fewer trees. Gorrenn took this a sign that water might be scarcer. He decided to ration his water carefully. Until he found another stream or other source, he would drink only as he needed, no more. He eased his pace, just a little to conserve his consumables. To Gorrenn, there seemed to be a direct relationship between how hard he exerted himself, and how much he drank and ate. He didn't know how this came to be so evident, when no one had taught it to him. He considered it one of those things that just was, and needed no real explaining.

Gorrenn thought more of the breakfast meeting two days ago. Assh had explained that the other families of the village would not tolerate Gorrenn living there any longer. He explained that what Gorrenn had done – what had happened to him – was because he was the child of a Warrior. Thousands of generations of marriage with the goal of producing Fighter offspring had resulted in special abilities being incorporated into their being. The evident result was what had overcome Gorrenn in dispatching a hugely outsized foe without hesitation, and nearly without effort. It was the special ability coupled with the easy transition from any condition into one of extreme violence that made Fighters. Exceptional skill and courage as a Fighter was rewarded with troop marks, and an opportunity to be a Warrior.

The obviousness of the nature of his abilities set Gorrenn instantly apart from everyone else in the village. Even while walking back to his home after the incident with Prodiggan he had noticed the looks on the faces of the other villagers. Fear. The next day had been even worse. All the people of the village stayed indoors except for working the fields. Gorrenn saw none of the children of the village. It was as though they were being hidden from him. His friends Jolangg, and Llakani were among the missing, nowhere to be seen.

Assh determined that the day after the beating of Prodiggan would just have to be. Over the very vociferous objections of Laeffas, Gorrenn would not be made to leave in haste. Time would be taken to prepare for his journey. Care and consideration would be given to their son. A day - for everyone in their little family to think of what they wanted and needed to say - was what they had to have.

Many things had been said the day before Gorrenn left Daffin. The farm work was let go for an additional day, in order that Assh and Borrda, as well as Gorrenn, could prepare for what had to come next. Early in the day, most things were said choking back strong emotion of one sort or another. Clothes were sorted out, food was prepared and packed for travel. As the midday meal passed and a bit of acceptance crept into their collective consciousness, more pointed, albeit calmer, things were talked about.

It was in the afternoon of this day that Gorrenn heard a thing that was truly heartening to him. "Your father named you," Assh had said. "When he brought you to us, he said that Gorrenn was the name he had given you, with the assent of your mother."

Borrda added, "He said we could use it, or not. We thought it was a good name."

"So, Gorrenn you are." Assh had said this with a finality that brought conversation to a close for a while. Even on a day of not farming, chores needed tending to and some work interrupted the likelihood of lengthy discussions. Even the kitchen seemed to conspire against the little family, breads, and sweet cakes needing tending periodically.

By the time the evening meal came, everyone was past saying the profound things they needed to say. The dinner conversation was typical of any other day on the farm. Assh, Borrda, and Gorrenn had all unconsciously sought out a little normalcy on a very abnormal day in their lives. Dishes were washed and put up. The feed-fowl, and animal pens were secured for the night.

Assh brought out his lute, one that he only played on the rarest of occasions. He sang a song from the Tradition of Natalis, the season after The Cold. The song was usually sung only in the first month of the year, the month when the Tradition of Grace was the focus of worship. The song he sang was one of reminding all that the life of man, and all creatures, had a place in the world. The song gave hope in a time of the year when The Cold always seemed to have dragged on too long, as it did, nearly every year. Borrda and Gorrenn knew the song well, and sang along.

Gorrenn remembered the night that followed as the most difficult of his life. Questions and confusion raged in his head for a long time, keeping him from sleep. He rose from his bed, a crept quietly out into the night. He walked to the border mark between the farms of Assh, and Stefirro. From there he could see the lights in Stefirro's house as they were being put out for the night. Someone had stayed up later than usual there, too. Gorrenn wondered if his friend, Llakani was the one. He wondered how it was that he had not seen either of his two friends that day.

As he stood there, looking at his friend's house, Assh strode up behind him. "People are afraid." he said. "Afraid you might hurt them."

"Me?" Gorrenn had asked, with uncertainty and protest in his voice. He never had any truly hostile feelings toward anyone in the village. He was not even angry at Prodiggan while he beat him.

"People fear things they understand poorly." Assh continued, "They seize onto one or two dramatic facts, and blow them all out of proportion. This makes you, right now, something to fear. The way you dealt with Prodiggan, told people everything they wanted to know about having a Fighter and Warrior in their midst."

The two farmers stood there for a short time together, listening to the night sounds. Assh put his hand on Gorrenn's shoulder, "Come to bed, you'll need your rest for tomorrow." They returned to the house, to their beds, and finally slept.

7

Gather men together,

or scatter them to the winds,

I will find them all.

- The Song of Death

The late afternoon of his second day away from his

home brought Gorrenn within sight of a village. It was not

the town of Ahngrist, as he had anticipated. Clustered near the side of the road, it seemed as though it had merely been tossed there by people who didn't care much about anything. His experience only with Daffin did not prepare him for the sight of the little village, apparently in the middle of nowhere. No animal pens, or outbuildings were erected near any of the eighteen or so tiny houses he saw. There was no evident place of worship. This really confused Gorrenn. There was no apparent store of any kind to sort from among the dilapidated cluster of houses near the center of the village.

Instead of being backed by tended farm fields like the houses in his village, these shabby homes, all backed to wilderness, bramble and woods. Gorrenn would have thought the place deserted, it was so drab, and seedy. A thin plume of smoke came from the chimneys and stacks of half or so of the houses, dissuading him of this notion.

As he made to pass by the place, a voice spoke to him from near the doorway of one of the bedraggled little houses closest to the road.

"No one much stops here." It was a young male voice, emanating from the eave-shadow of the house. As his eyes came to focus on the source of the voice, Gorrenn saw the young man clearly, at last. He was a head shorter than Gorrenn, and unusually thin in his build. His clothes were apparently selected so that they matched the drab exterior colors of the house. They seemed to have the same wear, and dirt as the house itself. Gorrenn's first thought was that, if anything, the young man needed a meal.

"Are you hungry?" Gorrenn asked. He was unable to restrain his curiosity about this first person he had met outside of Daffin.

"Oh, I've eaten plenty, today." Answered the young man.

Gorrenn stepped from the roadway toward the young man, so that conversation could be carried out more easily. As he approached he realized he had been wrong in judging the age of the man by his voice. Closer inspection revealed that the eave-shadow man was at least as old as his – as Assh – perhaps older. The light tenor of the man's voice had deceived him into making a mistake about who he was talking to.

"My name is Gorrenn." He offered his hand in what he knew to be the common way of greeting between men.

Holding up his hand in a "Stop" gesture, the thin man said, "Gorrenn, you say? That's impressive. Not the name I've heard on any man."

Gorrenn considered the thin man's reluctance to shake hands, and his failure to offer his own name. He had expected that things would be different in places other than Daffin, but just how different they might be within two days walk of his home was becoming a surprise. As his thoughts about the thin man began to coalesce, Gorrenn became aware of another small figure of a person, who had appeared at the corner of the small house, just to the left. Another small person, perhaps even more slight of build than the thin man before him.

"Jaeggo. that's my name." the new voice from the corner of the house was raspy and paper-like. It was a loud whisper. "His name's Ottgey." the newcomer smiled at Gorrenn, and stood away from the house to reveal himself completely. His clothes, as well, had been chosen so that he would blend in with the drab coloration of the houses in the little town nearly perfectly.

The thin man, Ottgey, became uneasy, and scowled at the figure at the corner of the house. Looking at Jaeggo, he said "I've told you before, you don't offer information, boy. A thief's debt to his knot, remember."

He quickly lunged toward the corner of the house, raising his hand as if to strike the smaller Jaeggo. The boy darted away swiftly, disappearing around the corner of the house before Ottgey could reach him.

"Better be fast. Not too bright." Ottgey muttered as he turned back to Gorrenn.

"Does your village have a name?" Asked Gorrenn. He was now even more suspicious about the ramshackle little village. He was also put on alert by Ottgey's behavior, and evident violent inclination, at least toward the smaller man. The reference to the 'thieves knot', the way that gangs of thieves bound themselves to each other, troubled Gorrenn mightily.

"Dirq." was all that Ottgey said.

Instantly, Gorrenn felt the strange feeling rising up inside him. It was the same feeling he had when he dealt with Prodiggan. "Dirq, Village of Thieves." was what he had learned as a boy. All this man had said was "Dirq."

Dirq was a place to be avoided, a place of wrong-doers, a place of thieves. Gorrenn felt the need to be very wary. He was here, in *this* place, alone. He also felt the need to be somewhere else. Unavoidably wide-eyed, Gorrenn stepped back. Wishing, more physically than mentally to not be where he was any longer, he backed away from Ottgey, toward the road.

As he turned to the roadway, Gorrenn was met again by the boy, Jaeggo. Somehow, he had managed to get behind Gorrenn without detection. His hand had been close to Gorrenn, it now dropped to his side.

"Don't touch him!" shouted Ottgey. "He's a Fighter!" In a heartbeat, Jaeggo backed two steps away, pivoted, ran toward the alleyway between two of the houses, and was gone just that fast.

Now, standing alone in the roadway, Gorrenn asked, "What makes you say I'm a Fighter?" He was aware that Ottgey's shout had caused several shadowed faces to appear in doorways around the village. The strange feeling was becoming very intense.

Ottgey, turned away, into the door of the little house. Gorrenn heard him say: "Your name says it." Closing the door of the house with a creak and a bang, he left Gorrenn standing alone in the roadway. The faces in the other doorways all disappeared, one by one.

No longer faced with any perceived threat, Gorrenn began to feel the steel-fire-lightning sensation subside within him. Standing there for just a moment, he thought about Ottgey's words: "Your name says it." He walked away from Dirq, a place he had never expected to be, as fast as he could without running. Things unexpected were going to be part of his new life. He now walked toward

Ahngrist, with truly renewed energy. He had a new mystery

in his head to deal with.

8

Make war. Yes, make war, or peace.

It does not matter. I will settle all accounts.

-The Song of Death

Even though Gorrenn had spent a good part of the late afternoon in Dirq, he decided to get as far from it as he could before nightfall. He weighed the consequence of traveling on the road in even partial darkness as better than being any closer to the village of thieves than he had to.

Gorrenn went on, until he could no longer see his feet because of the poor light. He came upon a boulder big enough for a man to stand behind unseen. It was a stone's throw from the roadway, and offered the prospect of at least cover from the roadway. He might have missed the boulder but for seeing it silhouetted against the gloaming sky.

Gorrenn spread his coat on the ground, on the side of the boulder away from the road. This was where he felt it would be safe, even if he was sleeping in the open. He sat to eat a small bit of his remaining food. The evening song of the crickets and frogs had begun. While starting to fall asleep, he wondered at the events of the last three days, and where it all might lead him. Unlike the previous night, no interruptions to his sleep overtook him. The night swallowed his disquiet, and gave him rest.

The morning of the third day came earlier than it had the day before. Even before first light, Gorrenn had awakened, pleased to have found himself rested. He realized that he had slept well the night before, even though his night had been interfered with by the rider in the night. He did not understand how it was possible to sleep so well when not in a bed, or even in a house. His journey into a new life was beginning to teach him many, many things.

Breakfast on this day was meager. He ate only half of what he had remaining, planning to eat only half again of what yet remained if he found no other food. He dealt similarly with his jug of water. There was more of that since he had been able to fill the jug on his first night at the stream. Still, he only drank what he needed.

His journey on the road resumed with the question in his head of why no one had ever mentioned that in traveling to Ahngrist from Daffin, one would first come to Dirq. It was something else he had never thought to ask, and had not learned it from listening to other people. He had not read it in books. Gorrenn began to suspect that there were many things such as this to be learned. He began to think that the most important thing to learn might be what questions to ask.

As the midday sun started to warm him to the point where he removed his coat, Gorrenn heard fast-approaching hoofbeats again. A single rider on a fast courser. As he rounded a small bend in the road, Gorrenn could see the man and horse more clearly. The man wore a dark brown set of clothes, and a hat that shielded the man's eyes from the sun. The hat was exactly the same color as the set of clothes the man wore. From his reading Gorrenn knew this to be the color and uniform of an Accord Rider.

The Corps of Accord riders was selected from among Fighter training cadres. The best riders were selected, and asked to volunteer for the difficult duty of carrying messages from one city of the Accord of States to another. The choice would remove them permanently from consideration as Warriors, so it was not taken lightly. Accord Riders were very highly respected in all parts of the Accord of States. They were known for delivering messages without fail, not matter what obstacles might lie in their path.

The Riders were protected by laws enforced in all States of the Accord. Interfering with an Accord Rider was punishable by death. Since the Riders were Fighters to begin with, the sentence was usually carried out immediately. Few stories ever came to light of Accord Riders who fell prey to any man, beast or condition of the climate. Most people made sure to give Riders a wide berth, and a clear path.

Stepping to the side of the road, Gorrenn made ready to be well out of the Accord Rider's way when he passed. He watched with fascination as the horse and Rider approached, moving together as one great beast. As the Rider came within distance of seeing his face, he raised his right hand to Gorrenn in the traditional salute of one Fighter to another. Hesitating briefly, Gorrenn slowly raised his hand, palm forward, even with his shoulder, matching the Rider's salute.

With mouth agape, Gorrenn watched as the Rider brought his horse to a halt. He had managed a maneuver in halting the galloping animal that Gorrenn would have thought impossible. Truly, riders knew what they were doing with their horses. Neither the rider or his horse seemed to be breathing hard, although they had been working together to move down the road at a very fast pace. Gorrenn began to understand how Accord Riders were attributed the ability to cover impossible distances in unreasonably short periods of time. It seemed as though these two could do what they had been doing all day–and night, if need be.

The Accord Rider spoke first, staring down at Gorrenn from his mount. "Do you not know a proper salute, Trooper?"

Gorrenn, taken well aback, answered, "I know what a Troop salute is, but I'm no Fighter. I answered your salute out of respect."

"Did you, now?" The Rider eyed Gorrenn closely, inspecting him. "The fit of your clothes, the way you stand, all say that you owe a debt to a cadre."

Sidling the horse a bit closer, the Rider leaned down from his horse. "You're a Fighter, sure."

Without another word, the Rider reined his horse to the roadway, and made to gallop on. "Wait!" Gorrenn

69

called after him. "What do you mean?" The Rider glanced

back, a broad smile on his face, and rode on.

Gorrenn wondered what it meant to "owe a debt to a

cadre." Was it anything like owing a debt to a knot of

thieves? Probably not. Gorrenn was beginning to learn

things at each and every turn he took. One thing was

seemingly more surprising than the last. Out here on the

road, Gorrenn thought, even the most mundane things are

new and full of questions, and mysteries.

The realization that his life back in Daffin had been

sheltered from the complexities of the world began to set

in. Another new feeling came over Gorrenn: He felt small,

in a world that was much larger than he ever thought

possible.

With these questions and new sensations vexing

him, Gorrenn walked on. The fall of his feet to the road

surface was lost in the sea of questions swirling in is head.

All day long he looked skyward, now seeing the definite cloud of smoke looming ever larger, rising, he hoped it came from Ahngrist.

9

The day of your birth, or its hundredth returning,

I care not at all.

The songs of celebration cease, when my time

becomes your time.

-The Song of Death

The waning warmth of the afternoon sun reminded

Gorrenn that tonight would probably be cooler than last

night. It was the way of Long Shadow. As he topped a

small rise in the road, his skyward gaze revealed that the stain of smoke on the sky now extended from horizon to horizon. This was his sign that he was close to Ahngrist.

His hike along the road brought him to a copse of trees that straddled the roadway between a rock outcropping on either side. The rocky outcroppings rose to steep hillsides abreast of each other. This seemed to Gorrenn like a gateway provided by nature itself. An unease settled upon him as he traversed the portion of the road bracketed by the trees. He realized that 'natures gateway' was actually a place where a defense could be established against a force of nearly any size. It was a natural funnel where large numbers of men would have to present themselves in a narrow, naturally limited space. Thinking this did not seem unusual, or out of place to Gorrenn, but the realization that it did not seem out of the ordinary did occur to him.

The Time of Long Shadows

At a place where the road turned sharply, Gorrenn came to the end of the roadway's narrow defile. A view of the town of Ahngrist lay before him. It seemed to fill the entirety of the valley floor between hills that rose several hundred feet high, all around. It was a sight which in fact daunted him. He had never thought to see anything like it. Smoke seemed to rise from every single building he could see. In the distance, now in the shadow of the surrounding hills, Gorrenn could make out the movement of numerous people as they went about their early evening activities.

The sight of the town caused Gorrenn to pause in his walking. His pause grew into a wait, for what he did not know. After a time, he realized he had let the sun set beyond the hills to the west, and now Ahngrist lay completely in the dark half-light of early nightfall. Lights shone in numerous windows, revealing that the bustle of town life continued. As darkness settled fully and comfortably over the town, lights shone in the streets themselves. Gorrenn had no doubt that the lights were provided by the town for the people.

After a time watching nightfall over Ahngrist, Gorrenn decided to wait until morning to go into the town. Moving back to the copse of trees, he set up his small campground for the night. Eating the last of his packed ration, he thought of the many evening meals he had shared with Assh and Borrda. Would he ever again? He could not dare to hope so. It seemed as though a spasm of misfortune had chased him away from everything and everyone he had ever known. His predictable life and regimented schedule of farming were gone from him. Now, new things were coming at him at a discouraging pace.

***

Before he even realized, he had been asleep, Gorrenn found himself waking, standing with his left hand around a young man's throat. His right hand was on the knife at his side. As he blinked awake, he realized that as he had slept, his foot had been nudged, he still felt the muscle memory of it. He had risen from his position of sleeping on his left side, and defended himself from this young man without a moment's hesitation. He had apparently moved even faster than when he had delivered the beating to poor Prodiggan. He began to realize he really didn't understand any of the things that he had recently done without thinking. He felt the fire-lightning-steel sensation subsiding, already.

The young man in his grip began to squirm, trying to get away. At 15 stone-weights, and a little over 4 cubet height, Gorrenn was considerably larger and stronger than the young man still in his grip. He guessed this little fellow weighed no more than 10 or 11 stone-weights, he was noticeably shorter than Gorrenn. Try as he might, if Gorrenn didn't ease his grip, he wasn't going anywhere.

Gorrenn looked him in the eye and said, "Are you alone?"

"Let me go!" The small young man squirmed and flailed, trying to break free.

"I'll release you when you answer my question. Are you alone?" Gorrenn released the hold on the young man's neck, but kept a grip on him, holding him firmly by the shoulder, and slightly off balance. He had visually swept the immediate area, ensuring that there wasn't an additional threat.

Gorrenn wanted two things from this person who had awakened him. He needed to find out if there were others around, and he needed dialogue with the young man in his grasp to lessen the tension between them. Even though Gorrenn had the upper hand, he wanted to give the young man some 'currency' in the exchange.

"Forty men behind me, in the trees." The young man could not restrain a smile that swept across his face, at the sound of his own words. Gorrenn appreciated the humor, and eased his grip slowly. He feared that as he freed the young man completely, he would simply take the opportunity to run. The youth eased back a step, but did not run. Gorrenn internally sighed with relief, he had judged the situation correctly.

"You move like a Fighter, is that what you are? You're not a Warrior, no Troop mark." The young man eased back another step, still apparently not completely at ease with the situation.

Gorrenn relaxed a bit from the stance he had taken to confront the young man, and slid his water jug out of his pack. Drinking from it, he sized up the young man a little more.

"I'm a farmer, not a Fighter, at least that's what I was." Gorrenn offered the young man the jug to drink from if he wished. It was a feeble attempt to further ease the tension between them. The young man accepted the jug, eyed it a bit, then drank. Handing the jug back to Gorrenn, he said, "Tojjer, that's me; who're you?"

Placing the jug back in the pack, Gorrenn said, "I've walked from Daffin, the village where I lived. I'm on my way to Ahngrist, at least for now. I am Gorrenn." He sat down, and motioned for Tojjer to do likewise. Tojjer sat without any recognizable reaction to Gorrenn's name. Whatever the thief, Ottgey heard in his name was lost on this young man.

"No great goings-on there. Been there a lot of times, selling grain with my father." Gorrenn was glad to see that even though the morning had begun poorly, the two men were now able to speak with each other calmly. The

common ground between them was now established.
Gorrenn learned that Tojjer's village was Quaille, a farm
village a day's walk to the south of Ahngrist. That made it
about a half days wagon ride. No wonder Tojjer had been
to Ahngrist Many times. The journey was a small portion
of the effort expended in carrying grain to Ahngrist from
Daffin. Since this was, like so much else, all completely
new to Gorrenn, the learning went on.

Gorrenn was able to learn a lot from Tojjer about
Ahngrist. The town was, as Gorrenn had been taught, a mill
town. The work done in the town centered around the grain
mills that ground the flour for baked goods to be made.
Since several hundred people lived there, Ahngrist also
offered things that the small villages could not. The town's
worship hall could contain about half the population of
Ahngrist, but Tojjer said that he had never seen it even
close to half full. People in town seemed to not care so
much about the Traditions. Gorrenn did not understand

why this was. To him, the way he had been taught, the Traditions guided men in their lives, every day. He did learn from Tojjer that the town funded the position of Kellar, the Traditions Keeper for the community. It was a full-time job, although poorly paid.

The Festival Hall was in Ahngrist, in a building that once housed the Plenum, the congress of governors of Central West. The Plenum had since moved to Partajann, to be closer to the center of the state. Partajann sat beside the Shield river. The Shield had once, long ago, been exactly that, a barrier between the lands of men, and the Giants. As men grew able to build canoes and boats and move into land on the far side of the river, its function as a natural barrier against attack by the Giants was lost. The name remained, serving as a bit of a history lesson in itself. Partajann, and the river were to the northwest of Daffin, two weeks by wagon, perhaps as long as a month on foot.

The Time of Long Shadows

Tojjer told Gorrenn about the drinking halls in Ahngrist, the people who worked there, and the people who were their patrons. This was all very far beyond anything that he ever learned from Assh and Borrda, his reading, or from listening to Stefirro tell of his journeys to Ahngrist. Tojjer also told him about the different types of stores, the open-air market, and the livery stable, where Gorrenn might find work, cleaning out stalls. Tojjer told a story of hired hand at his father's farm who had worked at the livery stable. If you worked there, you were given food, and let sleep in the unused stalls, or the hay loft.

As to exactly how Tojjer came to come upon Gorrenn as silently as he had, there was an explanation. Tojjer, being eleven Summers of age, was being taught stalking skills by his father. Tojjer's father loved to hunt the forested lands near their farm in Quaille. He taught his son, the way he had been taught by his father. Knowing how to live from the bounty of the land was more than a way to augment the food supply for the family. It could totally supplant the farm diet, if you knew how to hunt, and what to look for.

Tojjer had come to Ahngrist with his father on a grain selling mission. They had brought two wagons, with Tojjer being given the reigns of a wagon for the first time. His father had allowed him the opportunity to stalk game, at first light, this morning. To his very great credit – and something that might have just saved his life – when he saw Gorrenn asleep, under the trees, he first laid down his bow and quiver, and stowed his knife in its sheath.

After a while longer, talking with one another, the two men parted company. Tojjer would return to Ahngrist, by way of first retrieving his hunting bow and quiver. Gorrenn turned and bent to roll his coat, and tie it to his pack. As he stood to face the direction in which Tojjer had gone, he realized that he was nowhere to be seen, vanished.

Thinking this was a curious thing since both men were

going to Ahngrist, Gorrenn walked on toward the town.

10

The lives of men before you are shadows,

as your life will be a shadow

in the minds of those who follow.

- The Song of Death

As he entered the town of Ahngrist, Gorrenn made first for the Festival Hall. It was by far the largest building in town, and the tallest. He had attended several Festivals there. Some years, no one came from Daffin for Havazas, the Festival in the Cold. Havazas was an old language word for the Cold, now just used for the Festival. Even though Daffin was closer than the majority of villages in Central West, the severity of the Cold kept people away. Some Cold season harvests were stored, some lost entirely, waiting for the weather to permit transport to mill cities. In years when the harvests were lost, people died. Nature served as only the sternest of taskmasters.

Once at the Hall, he was able to set his bearings from what little he knew of Ahngrist. Gorrenn had come to Ahngrist with Assh and Borrda at the time of various Harvest Festivals. The road taken with the wagons did not pass through Dirq. It was a longer path to Ahngrist, but it was a better road. It allowed the horse-drawn wagons to move faster. His knowledge of the streets was limited to the path they had always taken, first to the grain mill, then to the lodging hall. The path from there to the Festival hall was a short walk. He realized now that his interest in what his family was doing was always focused in the extreme. He seldom looked beyond where their little group was and what they were doing. It was what was important to him at the time. It had been long enough since his last journey to Ahngrist for a Festival that even his meager memories of the town were fading.

Now, Gorrenn set about learning the layout of the town streets in earnest. It seemed very natural to him to want to do so. From the Festival Hall, he walked northward on a well-used thoroughfare of the town. It was the direction in which he believed the livery stable lay. Ahngrist was a mill town. As such, it was crossed by a number of streams that flowed from the surrounding hills. Every street in town crossed a stream at some point. A bridge to cross each stream had been built for every street with the need of it. No two of the bridges had any similarity to each other. It was almost as though there was a law against it.

As he walked the street, he realized that he had begun his day with only water for breakfast. Not yet quite hungry, he thought perhaps he would be soon. Shops and stores lined the street on both side for several blocks. Crossing the side streets, he made mental notes of what he saw at each.

Gorrenn's search was quickly rewarded with coming upon the livery stable. The sign painted on the front of the barn building read simply 'Livery'. It lay near the end of the street as it became first a lane with small houses on either side. It then turned into a lane into the woods sloping upward into the hills north of town. As he stood looking over the scene around him, he noticed a hand-painted street sign the read: 'Gravely St.'

"Sort of a joke, that sign. Used to be the cemetery up that way." The voice had come from behind Gorrenn. He turned to find a man in dirty work clothes, standing just inside the livery stable's receiving corral. He was unshaven, and leaned to one side as though unable to stand erect. He held a long-handled scoop shovel in one hand. He leaned on the corral railing with the other. Gorrenn thought 'scruffy' would be an apt description of the man.

"You here lookin' for work? No horse." The corral man eyed Gorrenn appreciatively. "Why stop here, if you have no horse, eh?" Gorrenn was not used to such forthcoming friendly talk coming from a person he did not know, but strode forward to address the man directly.

"I am looking for work. I was told you might be able to use a man." Gorrenn stood outside the corral gate. He tried to not look expectant, not necessarily knowing why.

The scruffy man walked forward, exited the corral gate, approached Gorrenn, and said, "Let's see your hands."

Gorrenn extended his hands, palms up, for the man's inspection. A quick glance, and "You'll do." was the response. That was followed by "Don't need any fancy men around here." Gorrenn had no idea what a 'fancy man' might be, but was glad to find out it wasn't him.

Turning back into the corral, the man said, "This way." he walked across the corral into the stable barn with Gorrenn close behind. Stopping at the doorway of the barn, the livery stable man turned and said, "First, you gotta remember, the corral stays closed. Now go back and close the gate." Expecting now that he more or less had already been hired, Gorrenn did so.

As they entered the barn, the man turned to Gorrenn and asked "Have you had food yet today? Can't work empty." The food was plain, but filling. The smells of the livery stable, though not necessarily conducive to eating a meal, were reassuringly familiar. The work began immediately after the meal.

The first thing Gorrenn learned, other than keeping the corral gate closed, was that the livery was run by Katosse, the scruffy man. Apparently, he was responsible for everything that happened at the stable, but was not the owner. The owner, Gorrenn later found out was one of the 'fancy men' that Katosse had mentioned earlier. Fancy men didn't do any kind of real work, or so Katosse said.

Even though the work in the stable would be mind-numbingly dull to some men, Gorrenn found it reassuringly familiar. There was, from time to time an awful lot of horse dung to be shoveled, but never was the work too long in the day, or tiring. The food provided was the same that Katosse ate, never anything unusual; never anything bad. The hay loft was easy to adjust to after a few nights sleeping outdoors. Gorrenn found the sounds of the stable were not enough to keep him awake. The stable's location near the edge of town provided a bit of distance from the noisier parts of town at night.

Gorrenn had begun work at the stable on the sixth day of the week. Three more days of work passed. He was surprised to find the stable did a fairly routine day's business on First Day of the next week. Business that Gorrenn could see all around the confines of the livery went on as usual. After morning clean-up was done in the stable, Katosse told him to take some time during the day for himself. Unexpectedly, Katosse gave him a small amount of money, in case he needed it for a shop purchase. He told Gorrenn to return before sunset.

***

As he walked about the northern side of Ahngrist, Gorrenn became more confident of his familiarity with the plan of the city. Katosse warned Gorrenn to avoid the area around the older houses near the town center. Most of them backed to drinking halls, and had little to do with the houses where 'respectable' people lived. Katosse had begun to warn Gorrenn of the dangers of other parts of town, but stopped himself, saying, "I guess you can take care of yourself."

Gorrenn answered this with a muttered "Yes." Thoughts of how he had beaten Prodiggan entered his mind without further prompting. It was something he felt a strong sense of regret for having done. He wondered how much longer the sense of regret would persist.

Gorrenn's meanderings brought him to the worship hall, near the Festival Hall. He had not gone to First Day worship, he had been working. By the time he arrived, the communal meal was over, and a single person remained, cleaning the part of the hall used for dining. The person was an older man, Gorrenn could see his grey hair and poorly trimmed beard. His clothes were clean, but heavily worn. As he worked, Gorrenn could see that his face and hands were dark-skinned. Gorrenn had read of such people from the islands in the great ocean sea. He did not expect that he would ever meet such a person. His interest in coming to the worship hall had been rewarded with an interesting discovery.

The man, who stood a half-head shorter than Gorrenn, turned from his work and addressed him in perfect Malitokan. "There's food left in the kitchen, if you are hungry." The surprise of his perfect language command was such that Gorrenn could only stand mute, in wonder at it.

Gorrenn's momentary inability to speak caused the man to put down his work, and approach him. "Can you hear? Speak?"

Gorrenn shook his head, catching himself standing dumbfounded before yet another stranger. "Sorry, your words surprised me. I'm from Daffin. I've never met an island person before." Looking about the worship hall, he continued, "Is the Kellar here?"

"I am Tullo, Tullowimle Basseen Govinti, Kellar of the worship hall, from the island of Betrukki." He held his right hand across his chest, and swept it forward in an exaggerated gesture of welcome. "This is the worship hall of Ahngrist, all are welcome here."

Tullo sat on one of the chairs nearby, and gestured for Gorrenn to do the same. "You know that I am from the islands. This is good. How do you come to know such a thing?"

"Reading. I've read many books. As many as I could get, at least back in my village." Gorrenn began a serious appraisal of the Kellar. "I am sorry I didn't speak right away. I'm still just from a small village. I've only been here in Ahngrist for a short time."

"Reading on your own is a tried and true method of learning many things. But with help from another, a teacher, we can learn so much more. The citizens of Ahngrist have funded the building of school for the worship hall. Think of it! Children coming to learn, just as they do in Partajann, or even Malitoka! Right here! The teaching will begin in Natalis, just next year. The mothers have arranged for the governesses of several of the wealthier families to act as teachers."

Tullo realized that, in his excitement, he had digressed. He had neglected what they had been talking about. "So, what is your name, then village-man?" Tullo smiled broadly, and sighed, relaxing quite visibly before Gorrenn.

"My name is Gorrenn. It's the name my father gave me."

Tullo's eyes brightened, "A Fighter then, or a Warrior, maybe. I see no troop mark upon you. You have the look of a strong, hard man."

Gorrenn looked down momentarily, "I was a farmer, with my family until just a few days ago. Now I am a stable hand at the livery."

"So, your farmer father gave you such a name. It is a truly great, important name, Gorrenn." Tullo pronounced the name with aplomb.

"The family I grew up with were not mine." Gorrenn began the telling of the story he had just learned about his father, the Warrior with unusual troop marks. He had to hold back emotion he was not familiar with in the telling. He felt uncertain as how he was supposed to feel when relating such a thing. The Kellar listened avidly, but said nothing.

Finally, when Gorrenn had finished his story, Tullo enigmatically said, "There are many things to learn in the world. Not all are in books." He stood and offered his hand to Gorrenn in friendship. "If you would like, I can help you learn about your father, and your name. Now, I must finish cleaning the hall."

Gorrenn took Tullo's hand, and shook it. "I would like to help, if I could. Clean, that is."

"Good!"

The two spent the next hours cleaning the hall, and setting the furniture straight. No more talk passed between them. When they were done, the time had come for Gorrenn to return to his duties at the stable. He was lighthearted on his walk back to the livery. Even though he now had more questions in his head than ever, Gorrenn felt

that he had someone who could help him get answers.

11

I take from you the burden of all things in life.

I requite you with quiet, calm, peace,

sleep, and lasting silence.

- The Song of Death

As the next week unfolded, Gorrenn began to come

to grips with the ways in which men's lives in the town of

Ahngrist differed from the life he had known on the farm in

Daffin. The gentle way of interacting between people was

something largely unknown in the town. The innate courtesy he had acquired from living in Daffin throughout his youth, was lost on people he met in Ahngrist. A more direct way of speaking was common. It seemed as though people felt that time could not be wasted on the forms of courtesy.

Gorrenn began also to attune himself to the rhythm of the town. There was the frantic bustle of the mornings, and the afternoons, which for some, seemed to go on too long. There was also the slow winding-down of the evening. The day's rhythm made itself evident in a short period of time. The pace of the town was more hectic than in his small village. People still seemed to get less done. His work at the livery stable had its own rhythm as well. There were more horses at weeks end, less on First Day.

The next First Day, Gorrenn asked of Katosse if he could attend worship, promising that his work would be done, even if late in the day. At first, Katosse looked at Gorrenn disapprovingly. After a moment, a bit of a sigh left his lips, and he assented. Gorrenn thanked him wholeheartedly, and strode off toward the worship hall. On his way, he stopped and spent his meager amount of money to buy bread from a bakery shop, for the communal meal.

Once at the worship hall, Gorrenn sat in the rear. One or two people glanced his way. One or two people stared in disbelief at a new face in their midst. Gorrenn remained quiet throughout Tullo's discourse. Belonging & Family, was the topic of this month of worship. He was glad that other members of the group participated in the discussion. It felt more like home to him than anything had in the last week and a half.

The rite ended with a heartfelt "Thank you, all." from Tullo. And people in the hall made ready for the communal meal. Gorrenn brought his bread to the serving table to find that it had already been set with several different breads. A frown crept across his brow.

"Wonderful! You have brought bread to sustain us!" It was Tullo, already finished parting with those who would not join the communal meal. He reached out and put his arm around Gorrenn's shoulder. "We do eat a lot of bread here, but please do not concern yourself. The food we do not consume here now will feed many hungry mouths later."

Gorrenn wondered at the prospect of people in Ahngrist who could not provide for themselves. This was outside of his farm experience. There had always been enough, if not plenty. The existence of people who would not have food, unless it was given to them, was a difficult idea for him. Gorrenn knew that there were many wealthy people in the town. He could not understand why they would not automatically provide for those without basic necessities. It felt like something was out of contact with the correct order of things.

***

Like the previous week, Gorrenn Stayed after the communal meal to help clean up the part of the worship hall that had been used for eating. He noticed that Tullo worked more slowly than he had the previous week. Tired, he looked tired to Gorrenn. Why the Kellar of the town worship hall should be so worn out, he could not fathom. Gorrenn sped his efforts so that he did more of the work than Tullo. When they had finished with the cleaning, Tullo sat heavily on one of the chairs.

Gorrenn brought Tullo a cup of water, asking "What can I do for you, Kellar?"

Tullo drank from the cup, sighed slightly, and said, "There's nothing for you to do, only time, time, time. There's never enough time."

"I don't understand. You speak as though you were an old man, but you're not."

"Betrukkis age a bit differently from those of Malitok. I may not appear to be old, but forty-seven Summers have shone the light of the sun to these eyes." This gave Gorrenn a considerable pause, thinking he not only knew little of the world, but equally little of men. Tullo drank more, put the cup down on a nearby table, and said "After you left last First Day, I made inquiries. There is a man you may speak to about your name, Gorrenn." He said the name with peculiar emphasis.

"His name is Parranck, Massodice Parranck. He is Second Commander of the Western Army. He has fought against the Giants. You will find him at the house of

Jenssal, owner of the mill in the north of town. He gives

Parranck sanctuary." Tullo rose from his heavy seat and

gave Gorrenn directions to the Jenssal home. His last

bidding to Gorrenn was simply "Safe journey."

Gorrenn left the worship hall once again with a

head full of questions. Why would he need to speak to an

old Warrior about his name? Why does an old Warrior live

among men who are not Fighters or Warriors? Why does he

need sanctuary? From what? Or from who? For now, all he

could do was return to the livery, and do the work he had

promised to do.

12

Measure time in days, or decades.

I measure time in lives taken.

The count is of no consequence.

The next life taken, is as the first.

- The Song of Death

Work at the livery stable had become familiar, if not routine for Gorrenn. There were even afternoons when Katosse left the running of the stable solely in Gorrenn's hands. Few would know, but it was just an opportunity for the older livery hand to nap. His somewhat sleepy returns to work in the late afternoons told Gorrenn all he needed to know about Katosse's absence. The work was not onerous. There was no reason for Gorrenn to feel slighted by the arrangement. If anything, the food presented at the livery stable's table had gotten better since Katosse started taking his leave in the afternoon.

Gorrenn knew that the third season usually brought the largest harvest of the year. This meant that once begun, the mills would be working late every evening, He had taken the opportunity to walk by the house of Jenssal on two different occasions to see the exterior, and to judge the level of activity. It would do no good to wait until Third Harvest had begun. He needed to make contact with the old Warrior soon.

The Time of Long Shadows

On the second day of the second week in Esirren, before the first wagons laden with grain began arriving, Gorrenn decided the time had come. He requested of Katosse the time to leave the livery early in the afternoon. The morning's work had been unusually light, he thought perhaps Katosse might expect the afternoon to go easily as well. Katosse had had few men over the years who did their work as energetically, and efficiently as Gorrenn. He was generally unwilling to release a worker from his responsibilities in mid-week, but Gorrenn was different. He had not provided a single disappointment to Katosse since his hiring. Katosse knew this to be rare, and assented to Gorrenn's request almost without hesitation.

Gorrenn made what he could of his appearance. He made sure that his hair was neatly combed, and his clothes were clean. He walked the distance to the house of the miller, Jenssal. While walking, he tried parse out how he would best present his questions. The afternoon felt hotter than usual. Gorrenn suspected it was just his apprehensions taking hold. He needed more than anything to find out why it was people reacted so surprisingly to his name.

As he approached the house of Jenssal, he took note of the fact that it was the largest of the houses on the street, as well as in this part of Ahngrist. The show of ostentation as a means of conveying power was not at all lost on Gorrenn. He strode up the front walk. At the elaborate front entry, he clapped the clapper loudly on the door.

The door was opened by a tall man, slender, but very well dressed. "Yes." He said, flatly.

"I am here to speak with Parranck." Gorrenn said as politely as he could. He suddenly felt the burden of overly-good manners upon himself. He did not know why this was, but let the feeling just be there, anyway.

The tall man's eyes opened widely, in surprise. He quickly said "Wait." And closed the door.

After what seemed like several minutes the door opened again. Within the confines of the door way, Gorrenn could see no fewer than three men. The tall man who had answered his knock stood between two of the largest men Gorrenn had ever seen. On his right, man at least eighteen stone-weights, and five cubets in height, on his left, a man just as large if not larger. The man on the right wore clothes like Gorrenn's, evidently for doing heavy work around the house. The man on the left wore lighter garments, and an apron. Gorrenn thought he must be the cook, but thought no less of his size.

"What is your business with Parranck?" Asked the tall man. As he asked this, Gorrenn noticed a man had appeared to his right, at the edge of the great house's front facade. A quick glance to his left confirmed his expectation that yet another man was there as well.

Faced with five men now, Gorrenn repeated his original statement. "I would like to speak with Massodice Parranck, I believe he can help me. My name is Gorrenn." Using his name, as confusing as it was, was the only card Gorrenn thought he could play. At this point he needed to get through the door. What would happen next – well, that would be what happened next.

The door closed again. The men at the corners of the house remained. Gorrenn suspected that one or more of the large men still waited behind the door. As he stood there waiting, Gorrenn wondered if he had wasted his time, wasted Tullo's time, getting himself to this point.

The ornate front door of the house opened again, this time to reveal only the tall man who had opened it before. "Please come in, Gorrenn." Placing that now-familiar odd emphasis on his name, the tall man gestured smoothly for Gorrenn to follow him into the entry hall of the house. Crossing the threshold, Gorrenn wondered what sights would greet his eyes in a house such as this.

The tall man led Gorrenn to a room off the entry hall that was larger than the house he had grown up in. He saw that the many couches and settees around the room could accommodate a large number of people. The artwork on the walls was unlike anything Gorrenn had ever seen. The paintings were like the art plates in the books he read growing up, but much larger. And brighter, the colors bringing the subjects of the paintings right to life.

Taken well off guard by the extravagant surroundings, Gorrenn was surprised by a small voice at his left elbow. "Nobody will hurt you. They haven't had a reason to fight." He turned to find a young girl, perhaps nine or ten Summers, at his side. Slightly built, and elegantly dressed in clothes that seemed ready for a celebration, she seemed to float just above the floor as she stood next to Gorrenn. A smile graced her delicate features. Her long blonde hair was neatly curled and combed. She was holding a small stuffed toy bear in her left hand, close to her chest, as though hugging it.

"Nagybbaj, leave the man alone!" Gorrenn turned to see the source of the stern counsel given in a commanding voice. In the doorway entering the room from another hall stood another large man. Although he was not taller than Gorrenn, he had shoulders broad enough to nearly fill the doorway single-handedly. Blonde haired, with a ruddy complexion, he walked energetically across the room. He extended his hand in greeting, smiling. Gorrenn thought it not surprising at all that the owner of a grain mill would be such a man.

Gorrenn took his hand, shook it. The large, ruddy man spoke first. "I am Jenssal, welcome to my house." His handshake was rock hard, but he did not try to squeeze Gorrenn's hand too firmly.

"Our house. Damanna says." The little girl, still at Gorrenn's side, spoke to her father. "We should always say 'Our house' so we don't sound rude or selfish."

"Very well, 'Our house', now please leave us to our business, Nagybbaj. Ask Damanna to join us when she can." Jenssal's smile broadened, and beamed, as he knelt to kiss his daughter on the cheek. He turned her shoulders toward the hallway door, and ever-so-gently, nudged her in that direction.

"Nagybbaj, Nagybbaj, no one ever calls me Delleyven." The girl disappeared around the edge of the doorway, and was gone.

Gorrenn was wondering at the sound of the name Jenssal had used as a pejorative to his daughter. 'Nahggy - Bye' was the sound of it. It did not sound like common Malitokan. He knew the name Delleyven, not uncommon for a single female child. It meant 'precious child' or 'treasure child.' His vacant look was reason enough for Jenssal to offer, "You know the old tongue, don't you?" Jenssal looked expectantly at Gorrenn.

"I never learned any of the old language. My village is very small. We read for ourselves, to learn." Gorrenn stopped himself from looking down at the floor when he said this, although it had been his impulse to do so.

Jenssal walked to the rear of the room, and gestured for Gorrenn to follow him. He raised one of the windows upward from the floor, sliding it into the top of the wall. Gorrenn trailed after Jenssal as they walked out onto a broad stone platform at the rear of the house. It spanned the width of the large house, and was raised up from the garden behind a height greater than a man, at least a man Gorrenn's height. Jenssal led them to a table and chairs at the edge of the platform.

"I'm sorry that I assumed you knew the old tongue, your name misled me. It is a name from very old times We call my daughter Nagybbaj, it means 'Big Trouble' in ancient Malitokan." As he spoke, a tall woman came from the house onto the platform, and approached them. "This is Damanna, housekeeper here, and governess to my daughter, Delleyven." Jenssal gestured toward the older woman. He had decided to dispense with the pejorative, at least for now, though Gorrenn.

"Just because you pay me well is no excuse for undoing what I teach your daughter." Damanna stood with a defiantly erect posture and faced Jenssal without speaking further.

117

"Does every one of my words and deeds come to your purview, or is there something that I might have said or done in the presence of my daughter that you do not know about?" Jenssal had now adopted the defiant posture from his chair.

Without changing her pose, the governess softly replied, "Your daughter's trust in me belies only that she knows there is no threat of tales being carried beyond these walls. You know this to be true as well."

Unable to withstand the determined onslaught of logic, delivered in such an even-handed manner, Jenssal demurred visibly. Without hesitation he said, "You're right, of course."

Looking in Gorrenn's direction, Jenssal set about making introductions. When these were done, he asked the housekeeper to have cold beverages brought out to them on the platform. He called it the 'teradsh,' another word with the old language sound to it.

While waiting for the drinks to be brought, Jenssal explained that his family had always had a tradition of learning the old language as a way of instilling discipline into their children. Gorrenn was interested to learn of traditions outside of the Nine Traditions, especially ones with such obvious benefit. He was becoming more and more intrigued by the whole 'old tongue' experience he was having.

The drinks were served by yet another person Gorrenn had not seen while at Jenssal's house. A young woman wearing light clothing, not unlike the man he had seen with the apron. She wore a waistcoat with short sleeves, and a small apron on the front of her pants. Gorrenn guessed this might be a uniform of the servants in the house.

119

"A lemon drink we mix with a little naccheo."
Jenssal held his glass as in a toast. "Jrravunikki."

Gorrenn knew of naccheo, distilled from grain, there was always some where the grain was grown. He had drunk it, but not taken a liking to it, having seen it do things to men's minds that were not right. He attempted to repeat the toast, "Javruniki" not the same but received with a smile from his host all the same.

"Our familiarity with the old tongue, and some of the old ways is part of why Parranck is here. The other part is family honor." Jenssal went on to explain that Parranck was Second Commander of the Western Army. Several years ago, two of Jenssal's sons, Drevves, and Cuffan, had gone to war with the Army. They had both wanted to become Fighters from an early age. No other course in life would satisfy them. They had been accepted for training and to no one's surprise, excelled in the skills of Fighters.

So much did they excel that they were inducted into the First Cadre of the Western Army, an honor usually reserved for veteran Warriors. They received their Troop Marks.

A short time after their induction to Warrior status, and inclusion in the First Cadre, the two were sent to the Aihvissuan mountains. Massodice Parranck, as Second Commander of the Western Army headed the column of eight Cadres, most of the entire Army of Western Malitok. Their mission was to drive the enemy from their stronghold in the mountains. They were to drive them to the south, or into the sea itself. There had been too many raids by the enemy, too many people killed. The threat had to be eliminated.

"Enemy?" Gorrenn asked. Even to this point in the story, he really had no clue whatsoever.

Jenssal, was a bit surprised and disconcerted by Gorrenn's question. He thought for a moment. Then he simply said, "Giants."

13

The breath I exhale is your life, gone forever.

The tears in my eyes, are the count of your days.

- The Song of Death

"Giants."

The word, delivered flatly and without inflection
left Gorrenn with no response. After a moment Gorrenn
began to realize that the cost to Jenssal of even saying the

word was great. He had long ago exhausted all emotion over the words used in talking about the brothers. Grief. Gorrenn had seen people grieve and knew the expense of it. Grief left people shells of their former selves, hollowed out, empty. Gorrenn knew now that the story would certainly be unhappy, if not utterly tragic.

The afternoon sunlight, broken into thousands of tiny points on the 'teradsh' by the sheltering trees, slowly crept across the sky. Gorrenn let Jenssal take his time returning to his story. Jenssal sipped at his drink, deep in thought. After a while he looked up and continued.

"The First Cadre always led the fighting. They were the 'pointy end of the spear.' The spear was eight Cadres of the Western Army, personally commanded by Massodice Parranck." Jenssal leaned back in his chair, as though suddenly faced with exhaustion. He drew a deep breath and let it out slowly.

"If you didn't know, the wars between men and Giants have never been anything but horrible. There are no prisoners taken. Ever. There is only killing. People here, in the middle of Malitok, know little of the wars. They don't want to know. Every generation wishes for their sons and daughters to not have to know about the horrors of war with the Giants." Jenssal's eyes were reddening, tears welling up.

Gorrenn hadn't realized he would be walking into this kind of emotional setting while looking for answers to his many questions. He had no idea of the connection of his name to the story that Jenssal was struggling to relate. He looked away from Jenssal hoping to give him an opportunity to gather himself again.

Jenssal took a long drink from his cup, and continued. "Men have been enemies of Giants for all time. If there was a time in the distant past when men lived in the world and did not know the Giants, it is forgotten. Men and Giants eat the same foods, and hunt the same game, to feed their young. Who knows when the first battle took place? No one."

"At the time of the campaign in the Aihvissuan, I was still a father who thought of his sons as boys, not as the men they had become. This led me to a grave mistake, one I cannot ever undo. I decided to follow the Aihvissuan column into the mountains. What my intentions were, I cannot say. They never really formed into a plan beyond being with my sons again. I left the operation of the mill to my wife, Genniel, and the mill foreman. And rode out of Ahngrist.

"Across the Shield river, I rode for one hundred, twenty days, westward. Most of the ride was across the western Great Plain, then into the foothills of the Aihvissuan. I saw the camp smoke in the mountains ahead of me. I used it to guide my path in following the column. Nearly out of supplies, I came upon the camp at mid-afternoon on the one hundred-twenty-third day of my journey. The column had left only a statute guard at the camp. I learned that the Cadres had formed in the morning for an assault on the Giants stronghold. They had marched and ridden out at first light of day. Before evening, the first Warriors were beginning to return from the assault.

"Massodice Parranck, on horseback, rode in with the First Cadre, or what was left of it. Battered and broken men limped and hobbled back to the camp. Looking at their faces, I saw only sorrow and fatigue, along with their winces of pain. Parranck himself had an obviously broken arm in a sling. I did not see my sons.

"After several Cadres had entered the camp, sledges bearing the wounded and maimed, pulled by horses, filed in, one by one. The younger of my two sons was on one of them. Covered in a horsehide, I could not make sense of the extent of his injuries. He was not conscious. As the last of the wounded were brought back into camp, a deep sense of dread began to overtake me. My oldest son had not returned."

The afternoon was growing old, the cold drinks had long since turned warm. Neither of the two men took notice of either. Gorrenn, far from growing weary of the long story, could not see anything but Jenssal's broken countenance, hear anything but his words.

Jenssal continued. "After a while, in the camp, I asked to speak to Massodice Parranck. A while longer, and an aide-de-camp came for me. By now it was well into night. I entered the commander's billet tent and waited for him to address me. The quiet around the commander's tent was unsettling. It was as though the rest of the camp, by some strange effort, managed to make no sound at all. I think it was my own dread of his words that grew the silence.

"Without looking up from the report he was writing, Massodice Parranck said 'Your sons fought well.'

"'The battle...' I had started to ask about the assault, he cut me off. Holding up a hand, he said 'Your sons fought well. You need to know nothing else.'

"No! I spoke loudly, with determination in my mind and voice. 'Very well, said Massodice Parranck, come.' He led me from his tent to a large camp tent where the wounded were tended to. As we walked among the litters and cots, he said 'Most of these men will fight again, not your son.' We arrived at the side of my son's litter. It was propped up slightly to elevate his head. He was not awake.

"Massodice Parranck spoke firmly but softly. 'If he awakens, he will be in great pain. His back is broken. He will not walk again.' He hesitated a moment, then said, 'His arms are gone, the Giants are foul enemies, they delight in pulling men apart.'

"I don't know how long I stood there looking at my younger son's face. His hair was matted with sweat and blood. There were many small cuts and scrapes on his face. A large cut crossed the bridge of his nose and dried blood trailed from the corner of his mouth. It was hard to see him breathe. He did so only shallowly. At last, I was able to look away for a moment, and looked toward Parranck. Until that very moment, I had seen the hard character of his face as being born of strength, courage, and determination. Now I understood it was the hardness of having witnessed too much death, too much horrible bloodshed.

"He spoke again, just slightly above a whisper. 'We do not let our Warriors suffer bad deaths. No death is good, but some are worse than others.' It took me a moment to realize what he was taking about: My son's death, there before me.

"I was only able to stand there with my arms limp at my sides, mouth agape. Before I could summon the composure to say any more, Massodice Parranck led me, steered me with his hand on my shoulder, to the entry of the tent. 'I will see to it. Your son will not suffer. Go to my tent and wait. He turned away from me, drawing his knife from its sheath. I left, willing my feet to move when they would not; making myself walk away from the worst reality I could imagine.

"I waited in Massodice Parranck's tent for a short while. I heard him as he approached his tent, giving orders to his adjutants. The business of the Army went on. He entered the tent, and simply said, 'It is done. Your son did not awaken, he did not suffer.' If I saw an even harder face on him that night, it no doubt was of my own wishing it. My sons, my precious sons, both dead in a day.

"I knew at that moment, there in the midst of this cauldron of death and suffering, that I had been done a great service. Massodice Parranck had ensured that my son died peacefully. Even though I now understood that countless other Warriors had had similar deaths, those were not my sons. Coming to full grips with the enormity of my debt to him, I said, 'I am a man of some means. Any service I can provide for you in the future, you need only ask. It will be done.'"

***

Jenssal continued his story, the sun now low, close to the hills surrounding Ahngrist. "My night at the camp, after the first assault of the Aihvissuan Campaign, was like a dream. I wandered out of the camp and back to my pack and cloak that I had lain aside before entering. I collapsed on the ground and lay there until dawn, not aware of anything around me. As the morning sun's first light shone over the ranges to the east, the Warrior camp began to stir with activity. Another assault, another battle, was about to start. I arose, collected my belongings and began the long journey home.

"I hunted for what I ate in the wilderness between villages. I bought small bundles of breads and meats from villages where I could. The ride homeward had become a test. How would I be able to tell my wife what I had seen? Could I say more than "They are gone?' Aware that my appearance had begun to suffer, I stopped at a stream to wash my clothes, and myself, before re-entering Ahngrist.

"After arriving in Ahngrist, I made straight for my home, still unsure of what to say to Genniel, my wife. As I entered the from hall of the house, my daughter, Delleyven – the girl you met earlier – was there to greet me. Hugging me as hard as she could, glad for my return, she called out to her mother, to join us.

"The look in my eyes must have belied everything I might have had to say in explaining the death of both of our sons. At a single look at me, Genniel collapsed to the floor of the entry hall. I ran to her. I drew her into my arms and held her, both of us sobbing. For as long as perhaps an hour we sat together there, in the hall, holding each other, and Delleyven.

"Even whispered truth, as bad as the truth I had to share that day, cut Genniel's heart deeply. Our sons were no more. They were heroes, but still gone. Finally, after one great sigh, Genniel fell unconscious in my arms. The house staff helped me get her to bed, the doctor was summoned.

Days and days went by, Genniel got no better. The blow to her mother-heart had been too great. She would not eat or in any way try to take care of herself. No amount of coaxing on my part, reminding her she still was a mother to a special little girl, made a difference. A month after my return from the Aihvissuan, Genniel was gone. The grief that had clutched her heart led her to will herself to death.

"I am here now, with my daughter, more or less alone. Damanna sees that everything surrounding my daughter is right, and that's all that matters to me. The day has gone by, I was hoping you could stay and have dinner with us. You will meet Massodice Parranck. I have sent word back to the livery that you will not return this evening. Katosse will have to get along without you for a night.

At the mention of the stable manager's name, Gorrenn wondered if Jenssal was the 'fancy man' who owned the livery. If so, it was an unfair characterization. The mill owner certainly was familiar with hard work, and plain-spoken. He was also very familiar with Gorrenn's working situation without having been told about it, at least not by Gorrenn. There were questions growing inside other questions.

Gorrenn accepted the invitation. He was more interested in meeting Massodice Parranck than ever.

14

When we meet, wherever, you will think it unkind.

Young, strong and hale; old, weak, and ill.

- The Song of Death

Parranck, Massodice Parranck was never addressed,

seldom spoken of without the honorarium Massodice.

'Great Commander' was in the name, it was a title that had

been earned. Twenty-four years of war with the Giants,

driving them back, back, and away from the lands of men,

had made him worthy of the title. He had been seated at the table directly across from Gorrenn. Both men took considerable measure of each other, while attending to the pleasant necessities of an evening meal.

Introductions had been made, and much small talk accompanied the meal, largely for the benefit of Jenssal's daughter Delleyven. When the meal had finished, Damanna and her young charge excused themselves from the room.

After excusing the serving staff for the balance of the night, Jenssal began the conversation between the men. "Massodice Parranck is here, as I'm sure you have learned, under the protection of my house. Even though you have learned this, you do not know why. If you remember in the story I told you this afternoon, Massodice Parranck did a great service for me. In return, I offered him repayment of the debt without reservation, or limitation.

"Massodice Parranck has served the Western Army for many years. In his years of commanding the Cadres, sending men to fight the Giants, he has sent many to their death. Too many. No commander has ever had the success in battle that Massodice Parranck has had, but it has come at an egregious cost in human life.

"Despite the fact that it has come at the cost of great numbers of Giant dead, the families of some of the fallen have sought to avenge their loss on him. If I had not been at the Aihvissuan camp, I might easily be one of the seekers-of-vengeance. Because of his service to our family, he is under our protection for the rest of his life. He is welcome to live here as long as he wishes.

Gorrenn began to respond by saying, "I'm sorry the Aihvissuan battles went poorly...'

"The Aihvissuan Campaign was a success, at least in a limited sense. We eliminated the threat of the Giants from the lands both east and west of the Aihvissuan Mountains. No Giants inhabit that part of Malitok any longer." Massodice Parranck had spoken in an even tone, not weighed down by the evident enormous death toll he was referring to.

"The eighteen Cadres under my command were fairly decimated by fighting with the Giants. They had made a great stronghold for themselves and it was proving difficult, costly, to wrest them from it.

"Naejj Atallon was called upon to join the campaign. We originally did not know of their strength in numbers. When it became known that the opportunity to remove that large of a number of Giants from the world, we seized upon it. Thirty-seven Cadres, nearly five thousand Warriors took part in the Aihvissuan Campaign. In the end, more than a thousand Giants were slain.

Gorrenn felt as though he only understood part of the importance of the numbers he had been told about. "How many Warriors were lost?" He looked at Massodice Parranck evenly.

The response was coolly delivered, in the way that a man who dealt with the hard facts day in and day out could. "Twenty-four hundred dead, seven hundred wounded. Of the wounded, only five hundred will fight again. Of the badly wounded, thirty survive."

Gorrenn masked an involuntary gasp with an exaggerated depth breath and long exhale. He let the knowledge soak in. One hundred seventy men, Warriors, had faced the choice to live as broken specimens of humanity, or die. They choose the latter, or it was chosen for them if they could not. The ways of the Fighters and Warriors were so different from everything else, it was hard to comprehend.

Gorrenn decided the time in the conversation was right for him to begin with his questions. "You know my name is Gorrenn. People have reacted oddly to it in many places since I was forced to leave the village of Daffin, where I grew up. All I know of the name is that my true father gave it to me, and that he was a Warrior."

"What else do you know of your father?" Massodice Parranck had asked with earnest animation showing on his usually stony face.

"Only that he had tattoos *and* brand marks on his face. He gave my family in Daffin village the choice to use the name or not. They chose to use it. That is why I have come to you to ask if you know the name or what it means." Gorrenn felt that he had poured out a lot of his life all at once to this leader of Warriors.

Massodice Parranck looked carefully at Gorrenn, and asked, "Why did you leave your village?"

142

Jenssal interrupted briefly, excusing himself to tend to his daughter's bedtime. Gorrenn began the story of how he had beaten Prodiggan with almost no effort. He explained the strange sensation he had while dealing with the oaf. He told Massodice Parranck of the other times he had felt the strange sensation rising up within him. He related how he was utterly bewildered by his expulsion from the village, his home.

Massodice Parranck rose from his chair and asked Gorrenn to come with him out onto the 'teradsh.' the moons were up already, crossing the sky in their eternal journey together. The 'teradsh' was lit by lights from within the house and moonlight. They returned to the table where Gorrenn and Jenssal had sat earlier.

As they sat down together Massodice Parranck looked at Gorrenn almost wistfully. "I would not admit it to myself until just now. You do resemble your father greatly.

It was not till you told of the tattoos and brands that I accepted the truth of it. Your father was a great Warrior, the son of a great Warrior also. His lineage in the Warrior family goes back generations too numerous to count. It is your lineage as well."

Gorrenn could only sit, motionless, unwilling to blink, or even breathe for fear that the words he had just heard would be true. The farm, and the life on it were all that he had known before being made to leave his home. Now, this terrible truth just simply could not be. The life he had known had turned to a course he could not have foreseen.

Gorrenn was unsure if he wanted any of what he was hearing to be true. Yet, he was getting answers to questions. In the face of such bewilderment, other people might become unsettled. Gorrenn knew that he needed information, a lot more information.

"Why do some people react so strongly to the sound of my name? It was the only name known of me in my village. It was taken for granted. What is it? Is it a curse?"

Massodice Parranck smiled ever so slightly, "It is not a curse. It is a very important name. Few people know of it. It is from the time of the very first Warriors. It is ancient Malitokan, the old tongue. Your name was given, I think, to call you to your rightful life when the time was right. Your name means First Warrior."

"You spoke of a strange sensation that has overtaken you when you are in dangerous situations. You felt as though your body were made of steel. At the same time, you felt as though you were on fire, and could move as fast as the lightning that falls from storm clouds. Yet you never lost your awareness, or ability to control yourself. Other men have felt this. It is the fighting frenzy of the born Warrior. Only Warriors who have long parental lineages experience this. It is the ability to fight like no ordinary man can fight. You were not only born a Warrior, you were born a great Warrior."

Gorrenn wanted to be angry, but he could not. He wanted to be proud, but had no reason to be. He previously had no understanding of where the violence within him came from. It was something in his heart, and in his mind, yet he did not know it.

He stood and walked away from the table and chairs. Confusion and apprehension clawed at him. He felt as though he had suddenly been caught in a trap. A tiny flicker of the fire-steel-lightning sensation began, down deep, inside of him. He turned back to the table. Massodice Parranck had followed him across the 'teradsh.'

"You must learn many things from this point forward. I knew your father. I fought with him in many, many battles. No other Warrior had his ability. He was the only Warrior ever known in all of history to kill a Giant single-handedly. His name was Harccosshan. He was marked as member of all Cadres. No other Warrior ever received those marks."

The evening was gone. The hour had grown so late that no lights shone from any of the houses around Jenssal's. Night had settled upon the grain-milling town of Ahngrist. Jenssal had lit a fire to ward of the chill of the night air. He had brought strong naccheo to further chase away the cold. The men drank together in silence for a time. Massodice Parranck finally broke the silence.

"You have had to learn many things this day. Hard things. Strange things. There is one more thing for you to know. I cannot let it go without telling you.

"I spoke of your father as 'was'. That may not be correct. He was lost in a great battle. No sign of his body has ever been found. Without that, no memorial was ever performed.

"He was leading the First Cadre of the Southern Army. They were given the mission of destroying the home of Giants that had raided farms and slain many people. The order was direct: Go to the place where they dwell, destroy them. Something was drastically different that day. Signs on the field of battle revealed that the Giants had set a trap, an ambush for the Cadre. Giants have never organized in this fashion before. The Cadre was slaughtered, nearly in its entirety. You know from Jenssal's story that the battle field, after the battle, must have been a charnel house. But no sign of your father's body was seen, nothing was recovered.

"You must understand that your father cannot possibly still live. The Giants do not make prisoners of men. They have never done so." For the first time,

Massodice Parranck looked away form Gorrenn as he spoke. "Still, men say 'He is with the *Orisoka*.'"

Gorrenn could only whisper the question: "What is *Orisoka*?"

"The name the Giants call themselves."

Take my hand to walk with me, or follow behind.

Either way, come with me, you will.

- The Song of Death

Part Two

1

Three things cannot be long hidden: the sun, the

moons, and the truth.

- *The Song of Truth*

The events of the evening and night carried the three men past midnight. Massodice Parranck retired to quarters previously provided for him. Jenssal guided Gorrenn to a bedroom to which he might retire for the night. He bade him a good night's rest.

The bedroom provided for Gorrenn was the nicest room he had ever tried to sleep in. It was one of Jenssal's sons' bedrooms. The furnishings reflected the kind of taste that would appeal to a young man eager to be out on his own. The things of childhood had been put away. Only necessities remained. If the young man had left behind any personal belongings, they had been removed.

Sleep, of course, eluded Gorrenn. His questions had been answered, but now his head swam with the answers. Harccosshan. Marked for all Cadres. No other Warrior like him. My Father. Warrior's frenzy. 'First Warrior.' The ideas, and the questions they brought, spun in Gorrenn's head. Hour by hour, the thinking, imagining and new questions went on. At long last, in the midst of this storm of confusion, Gorrenn fell asleep.

The morning found Gorrenn sleeping hard and much later than he ever had in his entire life. He arose from the bed in Jenssal's sons' room with a carpeted mouth. Naccheo. He had drunk more of it last night than he had in his whole life before last night. His stomach roiled. He sought out the washroom, and took care of cleaning himself up.

Still feeling a bit down, he found his way to the kitchen at the back of Jenssal's house. The large man who had been one of the doorway men yesterday, was busy preparing a meal. The aromas emanating from his cook top were almost too much for Gorrenn, but he managed to keep his digestive system under control. He was unsure if attempting to consume anything in his present state was a good idea.

"Come, sit, eat." The big man waved Gorrenn over to a table at the side of the kitchen. The window next to the table faced the 'teradsh', and the garden beyond. Gorrenn could see his host, Jenssal, with his daughter, touring the garden, animatedly discussing something of obvious great import.

Kaffe. Gorrenn had never drunk it. The large cook set down a large cup – more like a bowl with a handle – in front of him. Gorrenn took a small drink. His stomach roared, and he belched up some gas, no doubt left behind by the naccheo.

"Voices from your insides, messages from the interior, ha! Now, try some food." The large cook set down an enormous plate of food in front of Gorrenn. It was dripping with sauces and syrups of every kind. There were eggs, sauced with cream. There were sausages, slathered in dark brown, aromatic sauce. There were sweet cakes, absolutely drowned in fruit jam-syrup.

Gorrenn sat, and simply looked at the food. After a minute, he began to pick and nibble at the plate. Gaining momentum, he began to eat in earnest. The cook, arms folded, watching Gorrenn from in front of the stove, nodded approval. He came and sat at the table next to Gorrenn.

"Food, rich food will help clear your head, and your body. The naccheo can be treacherous, especially if you're not accustomed to it." The cook seemed perspire continuously while talking. After a bit, he returned to his cooking.

Finishing his meal, Gorrenn saw Jenssal and his daughter turn toward the house and cross the 'teradsh'. They entered the kitchen and confronted Gorrenn. "My daughter does not want to attend the school when it starts in Natalis." Jenssal held his young daughter close.

"I can learn from Demanna, just as well." Delleyvan literally crooned her response to her father. He looked at her with consternation and love in his eyes simultaneously.

"Please tell my daughter that the school will be better for her." Jenssal begged of Gorrenn.

"Whenever I studied with my friends, in my village, the learning was much easier. And, I'm sure Demanna will be one of your teachers." Gorrenn looked at Delleyvan evenly.

"You're on Pappa's side. I knew it." Delleyven stalked off, in a huff.

Jenssal's words followed her out of the room. "School, it will be!" and "The father teaches the child." The latter, Gorrenn was sure, was for his own benefit, as much as his daughter's.

Gorrenn returned to his food. Jenssal, who had turned out to be a benefactor of unexpected proportions, joined him at the table. The one ate, the other sat, and fumed.

"At every turn, she vexes me. Resists every attempt at guiding her." Jenssal looked out the window toward the garden, without seeing it.

"She knows you love her. I suspect that she uses that against you." Gorrenn sopped up the last of his sausage gravy with the last bit of a sweet cake, and ate it.

"I know. It will probably vex me more when she stops being difficult." Jenssal asked a cup of kaffe from the cook. "You came upon many new things last night, didn't you?"

"Too many. My head still swims with the number of new things I learned last night." Gorrenn carried his plate and cup to the washing sink, and began to clean them.

Jenssal interrupted him, with a hand on his forearm, saying, "There are people to do that. Please, leave the dishes."

It was all a new existence for Gorrenn at this point. He had always done for himself, He had always known who he was. Now, his life was vastly different. There was this mill-owner, benefactor, guiding his path toward learning about himself, his past, and his family. He was no longer just a farm boy, displaced to working in a stable. His family was important. By dint of that, he was, somehow, less unimportant of a person than he had been.

A Fighter? A Warrior? 'First Warrior'? It seemed like nonsense to Gorrenn. At least, he wanted it to be. There was, now, so much more that he needed to learn. There was so much more he would need to do, he knew that. He couldn't possibly be anything like all the things he had been told he was without having much, much to do.

Jenssal saved Gorrenn from being too lost in his reverie. "You came to learn many things last evening.

There is much more for you to learn, much more for you to do."

Gorrenn was about to speak when Jenssal cut him off. "I've arranged with Katosse to have your pack, your cloak, and any other belongings sent over. I took the liberty of having him informed that you would not be returning to work at the livery."

"Katosse told me that a 'fancy man' owned the livery stable. Would that be you?" Gorrenn avoided looking askance at Jenssal, but regarded him directly.

"Ha! That sounds exactly like something he would say! I am the owner of the Livery. The fact that you wandered to it on your own was better than anything I could have arranged." Jenssal finished the last of his kaffe. He plunked the cup down on the table, and turned toward the inner hallway of the house. He beckoned for Gorrenn to follow with a curt gesture.

They walked a considerable way through the house. The phrase that Jenssal had used 'could have arranged' gave Gorrenn pause to think that few of the things that had happened to him since leaving Daffin were without some influence from Jenssal. He thought back to how he had learned of work being likely available from the boy he met just outside Ahngrist. In his mind, Gorrenn began to suspect that coincidences were beginning to accumulate.

They stopped at a door to a room which faced the rear of the house. Entering together, they were greeted by Massodice Parranck. The retired commander stood over a large map of Malitok. The map was unlike anything Gorrenn had ever seen in any book. Rivers and streams were drawn with every bend and turn in place. Waterfalls and cataracts were individually marked. Every village and town on the entire continent was precisely located. Distances between villages and towns were marked. Every feature of the landscape that could be represented was there. The detail of the map was so great that it amazed Gorrenn. He felt as though he would be able to see people, if he looked closely enough. The top corner of the map showed a mark that Gorrenn had never seen anywhere else. The mark was a star shape, with crossed arrows penetrating it.

Massodice Parranck recognized the extraordinary fascination Gorrenn showed for the map, and the legend mark in the top corner. "This is a military map. The signet stamp in the top corner of this map is mine. This map was specifically made for my use. Unlike maps you may have seen elsewhere, the lives of men depend on the accuracy of this map. I have been working on scheduling Cadre movements to make sure all areas are protected. The Western Army still has not rebuilt itself completely after the Aihvissuan Mountains campaign. We eliminated part of the threat of attack in that area. We cannot allow ourselves to grow lax in defending land so dearly won."

160

"I thought you would be retired from the Army, Massodice." Gorrenn was uncertain about addressing the Warrior's age. He used the honorific as carefully as he could. He knew little of military courtesy. He did not wish to offend the great commander. He also hoped to not sound like a fool.

"I am, in fact, not retired. Although, retirement in these times of strife is a relative thing. It is true that I will no longer fight alongside other Warriors. That part of my life and service is over. I contribute my knowledge and skill in making sure that organizational mistakes do not interfere with the Army's operation." He made a sweeping gesture with his left hand, indicating the map, the desk it was on, and the room. "This is probably where I will fight battles from now on."

The commander left the desk, and waved Gorrenn to a pair of chairs and a table near the window of the room.

161

The window had a view of the garden, and several men could be seen working at tending the garden. It did not escape Gorrenn's notice that all the men were very large.

"We have much to discuss. We will do so now."

2

Truth is the only beauty.

- The Song of Truth

As the two men gathered at the table and chairs near the window, Jenssal excused himself. Leaving the room, he mentioned having to tend to matters at the grain mill, but in a voice so low, it was as though he thought it would not be of consequence to the two men. The Second Commander sat first, and motioned for Gorrenn to do likewise.

"While we are together alone, please just call me Parranck." He leaned back a bit in his chair, sipping at the mug of kaffe in his hand. "It's just so much easier. We have many things to speak of today, and formality between us will only make things take longer. For many men, informality with a person of my rank would be a burden, and a source of confusion for them that would actually make things difficult. You, on the other hand, have not yet been schooled in the structure of military courtesy and conventions. I suspect that if you follow the course ahead of you, familiarity with all ranks of men will be as natural for you as drawing breath."

"The course ahead of me?" Gorrenn could not help but ask directly.

The elder Warrior paused, considering what he was about to say. "You are the son of the most masterful Warrior who ever lived. More than that, you descend from a lineage of Warriors unmatched in the entire history of the world.

"The thing you must learn first, is that you embody the strengths of your ancestors entirely, it is the way our biology works. Your abilities are inherited directly, and intact from your father, who inherited them from his, and so on. This is the way in which the army of Warriors we now have has arisen over the millennia. Each generation has passed its talents down to the next without dilution or decline. This has much to do with the degree of success we have had in fighting the Giants.

"As the son of a Warrior, normally you would have learned much of what you need to know already. Your father, Harccosshan, chose a different path for you to follow before you began your life as a Warrior in earnest. I believe he simply wanted you to live your young life differently, and have a broader appreciation of why Warriors do what they have to do. I suspect he knew that your abilities would awaken on their own, and lead you to the ways of Warriors soon enough. This is at least my assessment of why he left you to grow up as a farmer. We cannot know for sure."

A wave of emotion began to surge upward within Gorrenn. Not wishing to lose the focus of the conversation, he suppressed it. There would be time to sort out his feelings later. He sat calmly, and continued to regard the Massodice with an even demeanor. In the back of his mind, he wondered if the preceding part of the conversation had been a test. He imagined many such challenges faced him in the very near future.

Massodice Parranck rose from his chair, carrying his kaffe mug to the window overlooking the garden. As he did so Gorrenn began to think of the presence of the Massodice's office here, in Jenssal's house. It was no longer a mystery that all of the servants in the house were large men. He knew now that they were all Warriors, here to protect the Second Commander of the Western Army.

By way of showing that he had been thinking, and not just absentmindedly listening to Parranck, Gorrenn asked, "Do your men, here, know who I am?"

Smiling a bit, the Second Commander answered, "Warriors usually know what they need to know in order to accomplish their missions. Too much information can sometimes be as harmful as not enough." Turning from Gorrenn to face outward toward the garden, he continued, "It may seem harsh or unnecessarily strict, even overly structured, but a commander learns not to burden his troops with information that might interfere with their mission. The men here guard me, and this family – you now, as well. That is their mission."

Now as intrigued as he could allow himself to be, Gorrenn asked "Were their Troop Marks removed? I saw none."

The Massodice stared a moment in wonder at the perceptiveness of the question, then answered, "They have all managed to cover their Troop Marks so they cannot be seen. Szavackka, the cook, is a Fighter, not a Warrior. He has served in many campaigns, caring for many men, and cooking many meals. His troop Mark was removed long ago so he could move freely in the world of non-military men. In addition to cooking, he has numerous other highly vital skills. Think of him not lightly. I count him no less among any of the men that I command. 'Shoulder to

Shoulder, all'." Parranck said this last with his wrists crossed before his chest, left over the right.

"Shoulder to Shoulder?" Gorrenn asked.

"'Shoulder to Shoulder, all.' It is the salute given to a new Fighter, it serves as recognition between men of fighting skill. It is also an oath to stand shoulder-to-shoulder in battle with the Fighter you are acknowledging. When fighters of equal rank meet the first signal is given with left wrist over right, the proper form of response is right over left. You will hear this many times, it is good to know how to courteously respond.

"We have spent a long time here, talking. Now it is time for work outdoors. Szavaccka fed you well, let's use some of that fuel." Parranck strode purposefully towards the door of the room without regard for Gorrenn. Following him was as automatic a thing that Gorrenn had ever done.

3

For truth to exist, it must be spoken.

- The Song of Truth

The ride on the wagon had not taken more than an hour's time. The little group, Parranck, two of the 'servants' from the house, and Gorrenn had ridden largely in silence. They were outside of Ahngrist, now, and far enough from any part of the town that they would not be casually seen. The field they were facing was backed by the woods that flanked the western side of the town.

As the ride out from town had progressed, Gorrenn had recognized the horse to be of the same breed that the Accord Rider had ridden, on the afternoon of his meeting with him on the road to Ahngrist. Strength, stamina, and speed were all bred into these animals. It seemed a waste to used such a beast to draw a wagon. The load drawn was not too heavy, by any standards, for the animal selected. Gorrenn thought that surely some other, less worthy, horse could have been chosen for the task.

As the wagon stopped, Massodice Parranck gave instructions to the two men accompanying them to unload the wagon. The men took three large crates from the wagon. Each was just big enough to be awkward for one man to handle. The weight of each seemed no strain on the men unloading.

While the men attended to the unloading, the Second Commander began unharnessing the horse from the wagon. It was reassuring to Gorrenn to see the Massodice pitching in to help his men. It seemed the way things really ought to be. Taking no small note of Gorrenn's appraisal of the situation, Parranck said, "When the Cadres work is to be done, all do the work."

The first of the crates was opened to reveal a very military saddle and tack for the horse. The Second Commander spoke. "You learned some things about who you are at Jenssal's home. Now you will get an opportunity to learn a little more."

The small group walked to the edge of the field, three hundred paces from the tree line. The first of the men rode the horse back and forth in the field, warming it for a run. "Keep pace with the horse." Parranck instructed Gorrenn, who began a trot apace with the horse, at an arm's length. The trio followed a roughly elliptical path in the large field. Round and round the horse and rider accompanied by the loping Gorrenn. Each lap of their course enlarged the ellipse until they were circling the entire field.

After a few minutes of this, a nod from Massodice Parranck, the challenging part of the exercise began. The horse and rider gradually accelerated. Gorrenn kept pace. From a trot to a canter, the horse ran faster. Gorrenn kept pace. He began to feel the effects of his exertions, but did not falter or fall behind. He knew the breed of horse could sustain the pace for a days-length if need be. He wondered how long Massodice Parranck would want him to keep up.

Twenty, twenty-five, and thirty minutes passed with the two men, and the horse circling the field. As they passed the point where the Second Commander and the other man stood, Parranck clapped his hands together once, loudly and sharply. The rider spurred his mount to a gallop. Not missing a stride, Gorrenn kept pace. The horse began to exhale steam-laden breaths of air, now fully in the run he was bred for. The afternoon air had been warming well before the exercise had begun. Now it was quite warm. The rider on the horse began to perspire, working to keep the horse in his gallop, in a field not well suited for the speeds they were making.

Once again, passing the Second Commander, he called out, "Full Gallop!" The horse surged forward, strides lengthened, the motion of its legs blurred by the speed. Gorrenn, now surprised at himself, kept pace. He was exerting effort, but now felt he could sustain it indefinitely. How long this would go on, he did not know, but he would keep up. He knew he could do it.

Three, four, five laps of their elliptical course around the field, the trio ran, and ran. As they approached

Parranck he called out one last command, "Now, Gorrenn, faster!"

Without hesitation, Gorrenn accelerated, outpacing the horse and rider. Being lighter of foot, he turned the ellipse ends at twice the speed of the galloping beast. Two laps into the 'fast-run', Gorrenn was half a lap ahead of the horse and rider. His breath was now coming a bit harder, but Gorrenn felt no inclination to slow down. Running like this seemed to be as natural as walking. He imagined he could maintain this pace for several hours, if he had to.

As Gorrenn began to catch up to the horse ahead of him, Parranck signaled for everyone to stop. The demonstration, such as it had been, was over. The rider walked the horse a bit while Gorrenn returned to the Second Commander. Warm from the run, but not by any means overheated, he felt good. He had not known that he could completely outrun a horse. Many men could outrun a horse for a few paces, some for a few more. He had bested the horse, and was about to embarrass the rider when Massodice Parranck had ended the display.

"You have just outrun one of the fastest horses in the world. This ability is the gift of your father, Harccosshan. No man ever ran faster or farther than he. His name, from the Old Malitokan, means Arrow in Flight, given him by his men. It is not only in fleetness of foot that your father excelled. Everything he did could be done at speeds unmatched by anyone. It made him the most formidable Warrior ever. You, as well, now have that speed."

Before Gorrenn could consider the implications of what he was hearing, Parranck continued. "The rider you nearly overran is the Riding Master for the Western Army, Dobitto." By way of thanking him, Parranck saluted Dobitto, who returned the salute. "Get to know him as well as you can, while we are together. He will teach you the finer points of military horsemanship.

Gorrenn was about to speak, but Parranck cut him off. "I know you are familiar with horses and can ride. Knowing so and doing so in the military is different. Your ancestor, Temmital, who you will learn more about later, bestowed upon you the gift of fine horse-riding ability. The innate rapport you have always had with animals, especially horses, is inherited from him. Your ability to run for an indefinitely long period without tiring is also his gift to you. Under the right circumstances, you will find that an unusual amount of physical strength is at your disposal as well. All gifts to you from Temmital."

Gorrenn was so involved with what the Second Commander was telling him, that he did not realize he had completed his run against the horse in the ellipse without much serious effort. He had returned to Parranck's side without breathing heavily at all. This was not lost on the Massodice, who called it to Gorrenn's attention. "You did not exert much effort at all in besting the animal, did you?"

A very self-conscious "No." was the only answer Gorrenn had to offer.

"Though you do not need to, we will rest for a while, before we begin again." Parranck sat on one of the crates they had brought. The light of the early afternoon shone upon the Second Commander's face. There must have been something different about the angle of Long Shadows sunlight that made him suddenly look older than Gorrenn had noticed before. Gorrenn wondered how long the Massodice had been fighting the wars of men against Giants.

4

Truth is hidden by belief.

- The Song of Truth

After having rested for a short time, Massodice

Parranck rose from his seat on the crate. He introduced the

last member of the group to Gorrenn. "This is Haditthue,

Weapons Master for the Western Army. His skill with all

of the weapons used by the Army is unmatched, at least for

now." The Weapons Master cast a sideways glance at the

179

Second Commander, tacitly acknowledging the slight. "He is also your second cousin."

Gorrenn nearly stumbled as he rose to his feet. A blood relative stood before him. He had no expectation of such a thing happening in his life. He was truly astounded. For a moment, he simply stood and stared. Haditthue strode forward, and gave Gorrenn a salute. Returning the salute, Gorrenn began to smile. His new-found relative reached out, clasped his right forearm, and pulled him into an embrace.

"Enough for now. You will find that many such relationships exist in the Army. Best to keep in mind you are probably always speaking to, or about someone's relative." Parranck directed their attention to the second of the three crates.

The two Warriors who had accompanied them opened the crate and began withdrawing several daggers, knives and short swords from within. Greaves, gauntlets and bucklers were also pulled from the box. There were evidently many more weapons in the box. Those were not removed.

The weapons were evenly distributed between the two Warriors. Dobitto wore greaves, Haditthue had the buckler. "Stances and forms." The words, given as an order by the Second Commander, snapped the two men to attention.

What followed was a set of movements that Gorrenn recognized from his reading. Battle Forms was a practice technique used to keep the body used to moving in ways needed in fighting. First, the two Warriors demonstrated one-man Forms. As the men progressed through their routines, Gorrenn felt his body starting to move slightly, mimicking the Warriors movements.

Battle Forms for two men required an initial armed salute between the two men, something Gorrenn had not read about. There were going to be many, many things about the Army he would learn. The two Warriors squared off and began an almost dance-like set of moves. Most of the moves were peculiar to the Warrior practice and not written about in books for general consumption. Gorrenn could not help but watch in utter fascination as the Warriors thrust and parried, dodged, lunged, and wove about.

After a few minutes the Battle Forms were completed. Parranck asked Gorrenn if he would like to try. Rising to his feet, Gorrenn retrieved a knife, dagger and short sword from the crate. He applied a forearm greave to his right arm. His left hand held the dagger. He added a buckler to left hand creating a combination weapon. The three Warriors all smiled and nodded their approval of his choice of a fairly advanced set of weapons to begin with.

"Stances and Forms," came the order anew. Gorrenn began, first with a bit of hesitation, then as his confidence grew, he moved through the maneuvers confidently. He even added the appropriate form for the dagger-buckler combination, pleasing the trio of observers greatly.

When his one-man routine was complete, his newly discovered relative, Haditthue stepped forward to join Gorrenn for the two-man Forms. "Do as I do, left hand for left hand, right hand for right; left foot for left foot, right for right."

, Haditthue began slowly. The pair moved through the Battle Forms routine. Gorrenn discovered that even though he had seen the moves only once, his inherent ability was so strong that he soon moved at normal Forms speed. The two finished and Haditthue congratulated

Gorrenn with a sound clap on the back. "Excellent, cousin! Ha' Aakka!"

The Ha' Aakka was a welcome Gorrenn did not expect to get. It was the call of approval, or positive acknowledgment between Warriors of a Cadre. Orders were always answered with the 'Ha' Aakka!'. His relationship with these men was beginning to feel as much 'home' as he had ever felt on the farm, even with the people he thought to be his parents. Change had come to his life. It seemed as though he had been swept away by the wind, and dropped into a new existence all in a single process.

The Long Shadow afternoon began to wear a bit. The sun's warmth began to diminish as the angle of sunlight grew more obtuse. The Forms demonstration gave way to sparring. This was done with blunt wooden weapons retrieved from the crate. The two experienced Warriors sparred for a few minutes so that Gorrenn might see what was expected when his turn came.

Gorrenn's first sparring session would come against Dobitto, not his cousin, the Weapons Master. The session began with a salute, just like the Forms demonstration. At first, Dobitto moved slowly and cautiously to Gorrenn's left. He struck quickly and repeatedly driving Gorrenn back several paces before he gained his momentum to return the thrusts and blows. As the match went on, Dobitto began to move much faster, and varied his attacks to throw Gorrenn off. None of which worked to undo Gorrenn's ability to stand toe-to-toe with an experienced Warrior in a sparring match. He matched move for move, thrust for thrust, blow for blow.

"You're supposed to try to win!" His cousin the Weapons Master called in from the sidelines. Gorrenn was roused from the relative reverie of enjoying his new-found abilities in practice-battle. He pressed an attack in earnest. He overcame Dobitto's comparative lack of speed, landing a series of forty blows and knife strikes in a matter of a few seconds. He drove Dobitto down on one knee. The match was over, it need go no further.

"Ha' Aakka!" Haditthue and Parranck both called out, signaling their approval of the match's outcome. Dobitto, flushed with embarrassment, had remained silent. Haditthue helped him to his feet.

"This is Harccosshan's son, remember." He held his comrade's arm and stared calmly into his eyes.

Dobitto looked at Gorrenn more than evenly, "Ha' Aakka! Son of Harccosshan." He smiled and shook Gorrenn's hand in friendship. "If you ride like you fight, there will be little for me to teach you."

The redness of embarrassment was now on Gorrenn's face. "I know there will be much for me to learn from the Riding Master."

Haditthue walked forward and gave Gorrenn the salute to start another round of sparring. In disarray from the previous round, weapons strewn at his feet, Gorrenn could only parry, feint, and dodge blows and wooden knife and dagger strikes until Haditthue had chased him around the makeshift ring, back to where his offensive weapons lay. Recovering one piece at a time in this fashion, Gorrenn finally rearmed himself. He could now return an attack pressed against him.

Fast, very fast, Haditthue came at him with such a multitude of varied attacks that Gorrenn lost track of them. There seemed, at first, to be no order or plan to what Haditthue was doing. Then as Gorrenn was pressed nearly to the point of collapsing to one knee, he saw it. There was a plan here after all. With a blindingly fast lunge, he struck Haditthue on the left, lunged again in a feint to the right, and disarmed his dagger hand. Pleased that he had seen through Haditthue's chicanery, he made to finish the bout with a dagger strike to left side of his opponent's neck.

In almost every situation, age experience, and cunning will overcome youth and ambition. Haditthue's knife was already at Gorrenn's throat, being slowly drawn across to accentuate the finality of the maneuver. Gorrenn's second sparring match had ended differently from the first. The honor of the Cadre, as small as this one surely was, had been saved.

"You were not ready for my attack. Always be ready. You saw the pattern of attack that I wanted you to see and ignored other possibilities, that is why you lost." Haditthue dropped his weapons, raised his hand in salute and said, "Ha' Aackka! Little Arrow. Yes, for now, you are

Little Arrow. Harccofenti. As long as you are training with us, you will be called Harccofenti. Now pick up the weapons, Harccofenti." He turned on his heels to leave Gorrenn to police the sparring area.

"Ha' Aackka! Little Arrow." Both the Massodice, and Dobitto chimed in, apparently pleased with the new, albeit diminutive, sobriquet bestowed upon their new trainee.

Gorrenn stood with his arms full of a stack of weapons, and asked the Second Commander, "I am to be a Fighter, then?"

"You are to be a Warrior." was the answer.

Walking away from the sparring area, Haditthue spoke to Massodice Parranck in a low voice, "If I had not thought of the knife move at the last instant, he would have beaten me."

5

Lose all other things, keep truth.

- The Song of Truth

The tiny Cadre sat and ate a small meal Szavackka had packed for them. The afternoon had begun to fade away. The evening was coming upon them. All ate in silence, water and an apple was even provided for the horse. Men of war took the care of their horses seriously, and small indulgences were part of that care.

After the meal, Massodice Parranck announced,
"There remain only two more activities that we will involve
ourselves in, today. Riding and work with the bow."
Gorrenn could not fathom why the group had waited until
the light was fading to undertake these two activities. To
him, it seemed that these two drills might best have been
done with more available sunlight. He admitted to himself
that it was a certainty that the intricacies of military thought
were not yet his to master.

Dobitto removed a set of heavy leather straps from
the crate that had held the saddle. He set about affixing
these straps in various locations on the saddle. Gorrenn was
unfamiliar with their use. They were buckled and
grommeted, laced through with leather thongs. Dobitto was
careful to make sure the fit and application was
symmetrical.

"The Riding Master will demonstrate the riding technique you will need to not only learn, but master." Massodice Parranck ordered Dobitto to begin.

The Riding Master mounted the horse and leaned forward to fasten his legs tightly into the straps affixed to the saddle. With a quick tap to the horse's sides, he was off, following the ellipse they had previously turned in the field. After a lap, Dobitto lay the reins loosely across the saddle and continued to ride the ellipse. He was controlling the animal with the pressure of his legs. That was what the added straps had been for.

With his arms folded on his chest, Dobitto guided the horse around the field, at a trot, then a canter, then at a gallop. Gorrenn was truly impressed. His reading as a boy and as a young man had provided him with no information on this truly remarkable skill. His wonder at the sight, and enjoyment of the moment were tempered by the thought that his turn to ride the horse would be next. He watched Dobitto intently, looking for every tiny clue as to the movements he was making with his legs against the horse's sides.

Parranck spoke at his side as they all watched the horse and rider. "A warrior who rides must be able to used his hands for his weapons. Otherwise he is just a larger target for his enemy. Fitting the straps for your legs becomes second-nature to a Warrior. He knows it may save his life, or the life of a comrade."

Dobitto slowed the horse to a trot, and began figure-of-eight turns in the center of the field. After three laps around the course in figure-of-eight turns, Dobitto did the apparently impossible. He closed his eyes. The horse stayed on a perfect figure-of-eight track. With his eyes still closed, Dobitto led the horse through the course in, and out the ellipse, in and out of the figure-of-eight turns. Lastly, he galloped the horse around the elliptical course, crossed into the center and stopped dead center of the field.

Parranck interpreted again, "A rider may not always be able to concentrate his vision on where he is going. If he truly trusts his mount, they can go anywhere together, with one set of eyes for both. This is military riding."

Eyes now open, arms raised to show that he was finished with the demonstration, Dobitto was greeted with a chorus of "Ha' Aackka!" from the trio on the sideline. He dismounted and walked the horse to the little group of men. From a rucksack he produced a carrot for the steed. The animal was indeed pleased to see what was obviously one of its favorite treats. It took the carrot and ate it heartily, with much chomping. Dobitto stroked the animal's neck as it ate the treat. A snort, a burp, and a little whinny were its 'Thank you'.

Dobitto held the reins out towards Gorrenn, "Care to try?"

Trying not to reveal the hesitation he felt, Gorrenn answered, after a brief pause with a simple, "Yes." He mounted the horse and began the process of fitting his legs into the guiding apparatus Dobitto had fitted to the saddle. Dobitto lengthened several of the straps where necessary, making sure of a good fit. "You'll learn to fit this to suit yourself soon enough."

The Second Commander cautioned Gorrenn briefly, "Don't try too much, this is not your horse."

Gorrenn looked at Dobitto, and asked, "Do you have another carrot?"

Dobitto reached into his rucksack and produced another carrot. He handed it to Gorrenn, the horse watching intently all the while. Gorrenn stuffed it into a breast pocket of the utility jacket he had worn. The greens atop the carrot stuck out of the pocket, and flagged back and forth. He straightened in the saddle, and took the reins. The horse, breaking its usual calm, looked around to see the carrot greens poking out of Gorrenn's pocket.

Gorrenn spurred the horse to action, walking at first, around the elliptical path worn in the grass by all the previous horsemanship. He managed to get the horse to respond to a few leg movements. His confidence in what he was attempting grew. His hands eased the reins downward onto his lap. He finished a third lap, controlling the horse with only his legs. Dobitto called out, "Half of the control is in the horse trusting you, the other half is you trusting the horse."

Gorrenn chanced getting the horse to a trot, controlling the animal with just his legs. Lapping the course twice, he chanced to close his eyes and felt the horse moving beneath him. He really felt how trust developed between horse and rider. He decided he would steer the horse into a figure-of-eight turn, and gave the command with his legs.

Before he realized what he had done, the horse ran at a tangent to the course they were on, and into the trees. A low-hanging branch struck Gorrenn soundly in the chest and unhorsed him. Landing with a loud 'Whump,' Gorrenn realized that the steering leg straps had given way in such a manner that he was separated from his horse, and not dragged along with it. He was glad of that. He got to his feet. The horse had stopped a few paces away. He began to assess just how badly his backside hurt when Dobitto, closely followed by Parranck and Haditthue came running up.

Seeing that embarrassment was likely to be Gorrenn's biggest pain right now, Dobitto shouted, "Ha' Aackka, Harccofenti! A truly memorable first ride!"

Parranck and Haditthue both chimed in, "Ha' Aackka!"

Absentmindedly feeling his backside, Gorrenn looked up and saw that the horse had returned. It now stood with its reins dragging in the grass at its feet. It was staring at the carrot greens still sticking out of Gorrenn's jacket pocket. Gorrenn took the carrot out of his pocket and gave it to the horse. A few hearty chomps, and it was gone. Gorrenn patted the animals neck.

Dobitto couldn't resist saying, "A few more carrots, and I think this horse will be yours, not mine." He swept up the reins still dragging in the grass. He began walking the horse back to where the crates and wagon were.

The Massodice said, "You now have wonderful story about your Warrior training that you hope no one will ever hear, Harccofenti!" He clapped Gorrenn on the back soundly, momentarily worsening the pain he felt in his butt. It was a good pain, a learning pain. He had no doubt that there would be many others. Walking a bit oddly, he accompanied the Second Commander and his cousin, the Warrior Haditthue.

***

The three approached the small array of crates. Haditthue withdrew torch staves from the last of them. The light of day had nearly completely faded. Objects more than twenty paces away were becoming hard to make out in the gloaming. The torches would be used, but for what, Gorrenn did not know. After his full afternoon of experiences, guessing what was next was not on his mind.

"We will only be able to work with the torches for a short time. It would be unfortunate to attract the attention of too many in the town." Massodice Parranck produced a Warrior's bow, and quiver of arrows from the crate. He handed them to Gorrenn.

Haditthue set about lighting the torches and placing them at apparently random locations in the field before them. Parranck pointed to the tree line at about the same location where Gorrenn had been unhorsed. "Haditthue placed a white mark on one of the third row of trees. Do you see it?"

Following Massodice Parranck's point, Gorrenn looked into the trees. The light of the torches in the field in the foreground flickered and wavered in the evening breeze. After a few moments, Gorrenn saw a faint mark on one of the third-row trees. The distance between the trees and where he stood was at least one hundred-fifty paces.

The third row of trees was another twenty paces deeper into the woods. The mark on the tree seemed to drift left, right, up and down with the light of the porches playing upon it.

"I see it, but just." Gorrenn said.

"That is your target. Shoot." The Massodice's voice was firm. He was giving a command, not making a request.

Gorrenn had hunted with Assh many times while growing up in Daffin. He had many experiences taking game of all sizes, in a great many different conditions. He had never tried a shot like this, though. He shouldered the quiver and nocked an arrow on the bowstring. He pulled the bow taught. The 'draw' of the bow was considerable, perhaps eighteen stone-weight. He aimed, and let fly.

Driven by the mighty Warriors bow, the arrow crossed the distance almost instantly. It struck the tree just below the mark made upon it by Haditthue. The strike was within a finger-breadth of the mark, but still constituted a miss. Deflated a bit, Gorrenn looked at the Massodice and said, "A difficult shot."

The Second Commander took the bow from his hands. He held out right his hand, silently requesting an arrow be put in it. Gorrenn promptly complied.

In less than a second, Massodice Parranck had nocked the arrow, aimed and let fly. The arrow struck dead-center of the mark on the tree. With cool, practiced patience, he looked at the young Gorrenn and said, "Sometimes, knowing a thing can be done is all it takes." Handing the bow back to Gorrenn, he said, "Try again."

Gorrenn took the bow from Parranck and nocked another arrow. As he drew the bow for aiming, the Massodice stepped in close and began coaching in a low voice. "Look at your target. See where it is in all the different movements caused by the torches flickering.

Know where it will be when the arrow strikes the tree. That is your aiming point." He stepped back.

Gorrenn did as he had just been told. After a moment or two of watching the wavering torchlight move the target, he got a solid sense of what the Massodice had just told him. He let fly, this time more confidently than last.

The arrow struck the tree, its point lodged solidly against the point of the arrow fired by Parranck, in the center of the mark. He looked at the Second Commander expectantly. He did not know what to say. He said nothing. The arrow had spoken eloquently enough.

"If one man can do a thing, another man can do a thing. It is time for us to return." The Second Commander began to collect torches and extinguish them. Haditthue walked to the trees to retrieve the arrows, and the mark upon the tree. Dobitto harnessed the horse to the wagon.

203

The crates were repacked, and loaded onto the wagon. The group of four men rode back to Ahngrist in the dark of night.

6

Be ready for truth, it comes only rarely.

- The Song of Truth

Arriving back at the house of Jenssal, the group was greeted with the news that there had been some sort of trouble. In their absence, a man had been found on the property of Jenssal's home that didn't belong there. The man had been apprehended by the 'servants' of the household.

Massodice Parranck gave instructions to unload the wagon, stable the horse, and continue on into the house as though nothing had happened. He gave Dobitto and Haditthue instructions in a low voice that Gorrenn could not quite make out beyond the phrase 'take care of.' He paused for a moment to speak with Gorrenn. "You have been born into a very difficult time for the Western Army. There are many complicated factors to be considered before you might continue on to become a Warrior."

Gorrenn was confused. The challenges of the day had been great enough. He was beginning to get a stronger sense of what Haditthue had told him earlier: "Always be ready." He had seen the Massodice receive the news about the intruder, and give instructions to his men without hesitation. He had a strong feeling that the likelihood of an intrusion had been anticipated.

Before parting company with Gorrenn, Parranck said, "I will need to speak with Jenssal. It is a good opportunity for you to eat. I am sure Szavackka has food ready, even at this late hour."

He turned and left Gorrenn standing in the entry yard of the house. Watching as the Second Commander walked around the end of the house exterior, Gorrenn wondered what 'complicated factors' might be. Mentally hitting a wall of unknowns, he made for the front entry, thinking of food.

Once in the house, he found it to be quite normally quiet. Damanna was giving an evening lesson to Delleyven. Reading aloud from a colorfully printed book, eliciting small rills of laughter from the young girl. He stood in the hallway for a few minutes, out of their direct line of sight, enjoying the sound of the governess' voice, and the girl's laughter.

Passing through the house, he was greeted by the smell of cooking coming from the kitchen. Parranck had been right about Szavackka, cooking for the men who had been away from the house, knowing they would return hungry. Being right, and consequently always being ready, were strengths he recognized in the Second Commander. Gorrenn was becoming more appreciative of them as time went by.

Entering the kitchen, Gorrenn was greeted with a boisterous "Harccofenti! The magnificent rider!" from the cook. Szavackka placed a platter of meats and cooked vegetables between Dobitto and Haditthue, both seated at the table in the enormous kitchen. Neither looked up from their plates as Gorrenn crossed the room to join them.

As he sat down at the table, Gorrenn said, "Magnificent rider?" He regarded his second cousin with false disdain. A small smile turned up the corners of his mouth. Haditthue chanced to look up, and broke into a wide grin, unable to contain himself any longer. The entire kitchen was soon filled with laughter.

The men ate their meals, able to do so now more as comrades than before. The Second Commander was taken a tray in his office, and ate on his own. Gorrenn thought this to be unusual for there was known to be little segregation of the ranks in the military. Leaders and commanders enjoyed the company of their men. The orders they had to give them demanded as much courage from a commander as the fighting of Giants did of all men.

Late in the evening, as Gorrenn prepared to go to his room for the night, he happened upon Jenssal, coming out of Massodice Parranck's rooms. A curt "Good night" was exchanged between them. That night, Gorrenn thought about his day of field training. He was too tired and sore to spend much time thinking about all of the small details of the day's events. He fell asleep quickly.

*　*　*

The following morning, Gorrenn arose early, as he had done so many days before back in Daffin. The first light of dawn was just lightening the eastern sky. Without the morning-after effects of naccheo interfering with his morning, things were about as normal as they could be. He was able to eat breakfast and enjoy it thoroughly, Szavackka providing a near constant commentary on apparently whatever came into his head. Gorrenn began to think of Szavackka as a person of simple needs who enjoyed his work as a cook. Truly, to have stayed in the kitchen so late into the evening last night, preparing food for late-arriving members of the household showed a real commitment to the work.

After eating, Gorrenn was again directed to the rooms set aside for the Massodice. When he arrived. He found the office darkened by heavy curtains drawn across the windows. The garden vista was no longer visible. The elder Warrior explained: There had been an intruder on the grounds. It was best to not tempt prying eyes with the sight of anything concerning the Second Commander's work.

Turning Gorrenn's attention away from the mundane details of the household and its surroundings, Parranck began a very pointed conversation. "There is a question no one has thought to ask you, Gorrenn. Do you want to become a Warrior?"

Gorrenn felt as if he had just been asked if he wanted to breathe or not. He had learned of his father only a day ago. The intervening day was spent training in military skills. His experience in Daffin led to his expulsion from the only life he had ever known. His departure had been abrupt. It left him empty. Traveling on the road toward Ahngrist he had begun to think of himself as less worthy, if not worthless because of what he had done. Now he was with 'his people' His people were Warriors. His father had not simply been a Warrior, but apparently the most significant Warrior of the ages. What had transpired in Daffin happened because of who and what he was.

"I can think of myself as nothing else from this moment forward, Massodice." He rose from the chair he had been sitting in. He stood before the Second Commander of the Western Army, and saluted.

Massodice Parranck rose to his feet, facing Gorrenn. "Then, so shall it be." He returned Gorrenn's salute. "For now, we will continue with Harccofenti, unless it somehow draws unnecessary attention to who you are. Your progression into the ranks of the Western Army will be greatly different from any other recruit ever accepted.

The reason for this is something you need to know only a little of from the very beginning. There are powerful people in the capitol who would not be happy to learn of your existence. They would be much less happy to learn you are in the Army. I will be guiding you in each step of becoming a Warrior. I have no doubt you will be a great Warrior, you will be needed as a leader sooner than you might expect."

The Second Commander returned to his chair and his kaffe. He let his words settle into Gorrenn's awareness. He watched as Gorrenn thought about the things he had just learned. He was happy to see that resolve and determination set the young man's chin a bit higher than hesitation and doubt would have.

"Starting tomorrow, you will spend each afternoon with Dobitto and Haditthue as we did yesterday. Each morning, you will receive lessons from your instructors. They can educate you like no other Warrior ever has been.

The things you will have to know are almost too numerous

to count. You will need to know them, no less." He handed

Gorrenn a signet ring. "This will be yours. For now, study

it, learn about it from your instructors. Do not take it from

the house. Do not give it to anyone but me for

safekeeping."

Gorrenn studied the object. It was a large finger ring

with a stamped symbol on the face of it. It was to be used

to identify documents that he, Gorrenn had written, or

commissioned. The symbol on the face of it was identical

to the mark on Massodice Parranck's map. It was a star

with arrows crossed over it. There was one small

difference. On closer inspection, Gorrenn saw that a third

arrow now lay over the first two. The new, third arrow

pointed straight up.

Things were beginning to gel in Gorrenn's mind.

He couldn't piece it all together. Harccosshan– Arrow in

Flight–Harccofenti–Little Arrow. Arrows overlaying the star. It wasn't all there. It soon would be. Gorrenn hefted the signet ring in his hand. It was not the sort of thing he was used to having or keeping track of. His life as the son of a grain farmer had led to him having meager possessions at best. In addition to a few books and an extra change of clothes, he didn't really own anything.

Gorrenn handed the signet back to Parranck. "Please, keep it for me. I am sure I will not be commissioning documents very soon."

The Second Commander took the ring from Gorrenn, and put it in a strong box in the desk. Pocketing a key that opened both the drawer and the strong box, he said, "Let us hope not."

Distracted by the presentation of the signet, Gorrenn had nearly lost track of the most pressing question in his mind. "Who are to be my instructors? Are they among the gardening staff?"

Drawing a deep breath, the Massodice understood that a good deal of explanation would be forthcoming. Forthcoming from him. "Your instructors are Szavackka and Damanna. They will be educating you." He let the words sink in, expecting the response.

"Szavackka and Damanna. So, I am to learn cooking and reading of children's stories." Gorrenn, considered that at least his afternoons would be productive.

Feigning impatience with Gorrenn's remark, "You have already learned to look for something other than the obvious from Haditthue. Both of these people are close to me. They would not be so if they did not embody an absolute multitude of talents.

"Szavackka is perhaps the most learned person I know. I know many learned people. He is by far the most capable. There is no subject upon which you might touch in your education that he does not master. He serves as the cook for several reasons. He loves to cook. You cannot change what a man loves to do. In that capacity, it is normal that he is always available in the household. Do not neglect that in addition to all this, he is a Fighter. He has not yet been asked to fight the Giants, but few Warriors would do well against him. His value as a personal guard is beyond measure." Looking to his cooling cup of kaffe, the Second Commander frowned.

Almost as he did so, the subject of their conversation entered the room bearing fresh, hot mugs of kaffe for the two of them. Szavackka set the service tray on the table between the two men. Looking toward Gorrenn, he was greeted with a profoundly mindless stare. He looked at the Massodice, who could only grin shamelessly. There

217

was just no telling what the old man had been filling the young Warrior's head with. Shaking his head, he walked out of the room, quickly, back to the safety of his kitchen.

Parranck called Gorrenn's attention back from staring at the door through which Szavackka had just exited. "Damanna is also very, very well educated. More so in traditional school subjects, but to no lesser degree than her counterpart. She is the master of every subject which she studies. Many years together have joined us into an almost wordless understanding of each other. No one has been closer to me than she. In the capacities which I have called upon her to serve, she has only excelled. You will find her to be most, uh, er, formidable. Actually, I wanted to say frightening, but it seemed out of place. You may decide which is best, eventually."

Gorrenn wasn't sure if the Massodice was in love with or terrified by the woman he had just described.

218

Gorrenn considered the woman he had seen teaching, and cajoling the daughter of Jenssal. He now understood that the image he had of her was the image that she wanted him to have. Just another governess. Not so. What other abilities did she have that Parranck was not being forthcoming with?

"There is one more important quality about both of your instructors you must know. Neither of them will ever be dishonest with you. In Szavackka's case it is a matter of honor and love for what he does. Damanna cannot lie, misinform or deceive. It is literally bred into her, a side benefit of the lineage which produced her intellect. You have heard her bring 'truth to power' in her conversations with Jenssal. It is a matter of every breath for her, her life. If either of these people tell you a thing, no matter how impossible or unlikely, it is true.

Stretching out, just a bit in his chair the elder soldier offered, "Today, I think it would be best for you to take time for yourself. You have been made to deal with a great many new things, all at once. This is the time for you to be on your own, collect your thoughts. Opportunities for time like this will be few and far between, if your future with the Army is to continue. For the rest of the day, do as you wish." The Massodice set his kaffe mug down firmly, scowling at it. The movement had a definite sense of finality. Their session together, this morning, was over.

Rising from his chair, Gorrenn left the room. He considered the 'if' his commander had just thrown down before him.

7

The inspection of truth reveals only truth.

- The Song of Truth

Gorrenn walked through the large house considering the Second Commander's words, "If your future with the Army is to continue." The words had come like a basin of cold water thrown in his face. He began to get a sense of how making any assumptions, or taking anything for granted, was now a very serious mistake to make in his new life. Just within the last couple of days he had seen and done many new things. The Massodice was right again. He needed time to process things. He would have to consider the meaning and import of everything he had experienced since arriving in Ahngrist.

Gorrenn returned to his room and retrieved his jacket. He decided to leave the house by way of the kitchen. Passing through the kitchen, Gorrenn left a brief "Good-bye" with Szavackka, who barely looked up from his cooking. He regarded the cook differently, but didn't think now would be a good time to get into the new relationship with his instructor.

Passing through the garden, he saw now that the 'gardeners' were obviously all Warriors. Each worked singularly, in a different area of the garden, spaced at intervals providing them with a view which collectively covered the entire grounds. The men were practiced in what they were doing. It appeared that they actually were working. Only a person who watched for hours would realize that nothing actually changed in the garden.

Gorrenn looked at each man, cataloging faces. He thought that he would probably have to know all these men before long. His new life, preparing to become one of them would place many such burdens on him. He came upon his second cousin, Haditthue, just as he was leaving the grounds surrounding the house. The Warrior asked Gorrenn, "Going for a walk about town?"

"Yes, come along. I would like the company. I have many questions for you." Gorrenn looked at him anticipating he would accept the invitation.

"That will not be possible, right now. I have been given duties that I must attend to before I can leave the grounds." Haditthue put his hand on his cousin's shoulder. "We will get to those questions of yours, soon."

Gorrenn smiled and turned to leave. Haditthue tugged a bit at him, holding his shoulder. He looked at Gorrenn intently. "Keep your eyes open, Harccofenti. Know what it is you see, who you see. Things are very different from what you have thought they were." He let go of his young cousin.

Gorrenn turned away, and left the property by way of the service drive at the rear of Jenssal's house. He turned toward the center of town. The walk in the warm morning sun was refreshing. In a way it was reassuring to Gorrenn to know that despite all the changes he had gone through, the life of the town went on just the same.

Half a block from the edge of the residential section, Gorrenn wondered what had become of the man found on Jenssal's property. Being completely uneducated in military ways, he had no answer. It was a thing that would remain mysterious to him until he learned the truth of it. He continued on, weighing this, and many other things in his head as he walked.

Not really having a destination in mind, Gorrenn let his feet guide him. He felt that, for a while, it was as good a way of navigating as any other. After a bit he looked up to find himself in the town center, more or less where he had wanted to go. The difference was that here, under the bright morning sunlight, the plainness of a grain mill town stood out above all other qualities. Walking from one block to another, Gorrenn subconsciously guided himself back to the Livery.

Wanting to say a proper good-bye to Katosse, he walked into the office of the stable. On his way in, he had seen another young man pitching hay to the loft. Gorrenn was pleased to see that a ready replacement had been found for him.

The Time of Long Shadows

The man in the office was not Katosse, but introduced himself as Petraddo, manager of the Livery. Gorrenn asked what had happened to Katosse. The man said he knew no such name, and claimed to have been manager of the stable for the last three years. Appalled by a man lying to him, Gorrenn could only leave. He did not know why people would act this way. What could be the reason for this chicanery?

Walking away from the stable, he chanced to see the hired hand – his replacement- staring at him. No expression on his face, he just stared. After a bit, he returned to his hay pitching. Gorrenn continued his walk about town, deep in thought about what he had just encountered. The sun had risen high into the sky, and Gorrenn found himself on the street of drinking halls. He passed one after another, closed in the earlier hours of the day.

Coming to a corner or the street that led to yet another block of drinking halls, he was surprised to find one not only unshuttered from the light of day, but in full operation. Music poured forth from the doorway. It was neither the songs he had learned to sing in his youth, or any of the great musical compositions. It rollicked and bounced, thrilled and piqued. Gorrenn had heard nothing like it before.

The sound of the music wasn't the only thing pouring out of the door. A sickly-sweet mixture of banca smoke and the unmistakable odor of naccheo, in great quantities both, issued forth into the street. Gorrenn had known the consumption of naccheo, it wasn't unusual at all. He had known Assh to occasionally bowl some banca in his pipe and smoke it. Consumption of both on this scale was very new to him. Stepping up onto the drinking hall's stoop, Gorrenn looked inside.

The sight that greeted his eyes was unlike anything he could have imagined. There were men in all states of naccheo drunkenness. The pall of banca smoke made it difficult to see into the establishment even as far as the back of the room. The women wore clothes that were so very strange. Brightly colored and revealing, to say the least. The thick, acrid cloud of banca smoke burned Gorrenn's eyes. He backed away from the door.

"Watch where you're going!" Gorrenn heard the words as his heel came down on another foot, behind him. The loud music roaring out the doorway of the drinking hall had masked the sound of someone approaching from behind. Almost simultaneously, he felt a small hand enter the pocket of his pants. Turning very quickly, he grabbed the wrist attached to the hand in his pocket and held it in an iron-like grip.

"Ow! You're hurting me!" The voice belonged to a petite young woman dressed like the women Gorrenn had just seen through the door of the drinking hall. The dress was all color and flash, what there was of it. Areas of the young woman's chest were exposed to an extent that Gorrenn had not ever seen. She squirmed and squealed, complaining bitterly about being held so firmly.

"Your hand was in my pocket. I'm sure it didn't belong there. Perhaps it was a mistake on your part." The young woman said nothing. She looked at Gorrenn with a hateful glare and continued to struggle against his grasp. The young woman realized she would not break his grip. She began kicking at Gorrenn's legs hoping to strike him hard enough to let go of her.

Gorrenn began to dance and weave a bit, dodging the kicks. Most of the young woman's efforts were in vain. Each blow that landed was as futile as the ones that missed.

Her wasted efforts made her angrier than she already had been. She began to protest quite loudly. Gorrenn began to tire of the episode and stood erect, raising his hand high, lifting the young woman off the stoop. As he did so, his back touched the jamb of the doorway behind him. He suddenly became aware that a knife had been placed against the right side of his throat by an unseen person who must have been standing just inside the doorway.

"Let the lady go." A male voice, evidently attached to the other end of the knife, spoke in a low, harsh gravely tone from behind him. Gorrenn thought the tone of voice was meant to sound like a growl.

Instantly consumed by the 'steel, and fire, and lightning' sensation, he quickly dove slightly to the left, grabbed the wrist of the knife-holding hand and propelled its owner out into the street. This was all done without releasing his grip on the young girl, who stood with her mouth agape in amazement. A display of physical strength and speed such as she had just witnessed had never been seen in Ahngrist.

The knife-bearer had only just stopped moving from being thrown bodily into the street, when two more men appeared at the door of the drinking hall. As they emerged, eyes glaring intently at Gorrenn, knives in their hands, Gorrenn released the young girl from his grasp. She bolted through the door of the drinking hall as if she were on fire.

Gorrenn was able to deal freely with the two men, now that both hands were available. In a matter of seconds, he had broken the charge of the first of the two new assailants by snapping his collar bone. He held the second man by the throat, choking the life out of him. Neither had been prepared for the speed with which Gorrenn had moved, or the strength he commanded.

Three more men appeared in the drinking hall doorway, all moving with intent, towards Gorrenn. He felt the man in his grasp go limp. He dropped him to the stoop, between himself and his new assailants. He had already planned his strategy to dispatch the trio, when they froze, and stood motionless before Gorrenn. They looked beyond him.

"Gorrenn, stop. Now." It was Haditthue's voice. Gorrenn turned just enough to see his cousin, and another man from Jenssal's house. Both were armed with bows, arrows nocked in the strings. Drawn taught, the bows were aimed at the trio that had just emerged from the doorway. Each bowman had several arrows in their bow hand, ready to fire a fusillade if needed. The bowstring hand of Haditthue held small dagger blades between the fingers of the third and fourth, and fourth and fifth fingers. Haditthue was additionally arrayed with two full quivers of arrows crossed on his back, and a spare bow strung across his back. He had knives and daggers visible on every part of his person. No fewer than twenty sharp-pointed weapons were present. The Weapons Master of the Western Army looked every bit the part.

A slight movement of Haditthue's bow indicating what to do caused the three men to drop their knives to the stoop. "Step over here, cousin." Haditthue and his comrade continued to watch the three men carefully. As Gorrenn reached his side, they began to back away from the entry to the drinking hall. Finally reaching a safe distance, Haditthue eased his bow, but did not drop the arrow's nock from the bowstring.

Gorrenn and his two "rescuers" left the drinking hall district as quickly as they could. As they returned to the residential neighborhoods, Haditthue donned a cloak to conceal his many weapons. Stopping the small group in the middle of a block, Gorrenn attempted to chastise his second cousin. "I would have taken care of those men." He looked at Haditthue with feigned contempt.

Stopping in their quick-walk back to Jenssal's house, Haditthue calmly spoke to his young relative. "Two important things you must keep in mind: First, you did not know how many men would emerge from that door. The next group could have been five, or ten. That was all a trap set by the drinking hall owners to relieve you of your money, and your life if need be. Secondly, I do not doubt that you would still be standing back there, breaking men's bodies, but a pile of bodies in Ahngrist is not what the Massodice wants for anyone right now. We are charged with the responsibility of causing as little disturbance as possible, while we are in Ahngrist."

The three men made a quick return to the relatively tame, familiar surroundings of Jenssal's house. Gorrenn was left to wonder, as they did, if he had somehow caused problems for the Second Commander. Complexities heaped upon mysteries seemed to Gorrenn to be the order of life as a Warrior.

8

Truth will be, whether you see it or not.

Truth will be, whether you hear it or not.

Truth will be, whether you know it or not.

- The Song of Truth

The long talk began on Gorrenn's arrival back at the house. In his office at Jenssal's house, the Second Commander sat in the chair behind the desk. Gorrenn noticed that the act was heavier than it should have been.

He also did not miss the fact that, whatever the content of this meeting would turn out to be, the Massodice had positioned them with the desk intervening. The map had been rolled to one side of the desk. The broad flat surface of the desk was interrupted only by the lamp on the other side.

Beginning with a deliberately slow breath, Massodice Parranck appraised Gorrenn coolly. "Your encounter at the drinking hall had the potential to undo a great many good things that have recently been accomplished. It is my fault that along with giving you time to yourself, I did not warn you about drawing attention to yourself."

"I'm sorry, Massodice. I didn't realize the danger, merely standing in the doorway could lead to." Gorrenn was honestly contrite, wringing his hands slightly while he spoke. "I wouldn't..."

Parranck raised a hand, "As I said, the fault is mine. My sense of generosity toward you nearly undid us. The only right thing that I did was to send Haditthue, and Meddace to look after you.

"From this point forward we – you and I – will have to exercise more discipline. It is for this reason that I am going to explain things to you that few other men know. One thing is that Naejj Atallon, First Commander of the Western Army knows everything in as much detail as I can provide him. Accord Riders are sent with dispatches as often as our need for attracting little attention allows.

"The nearly overwhelming sensation you experience – the one which originally caused you to be here – is Warrior frenzy. It is a quality that a person is either born with or is not. Notice that I said person. There are women Warriors. This is not a secret, but it is not widely known. You can master it. You do not become a Warrior until you master it. It is the quality of trained Fighters who become Warriors, and slay Giants."

Gorrenn mouthed the word 'women' without sound. This was surprising to learn, but then again, since leaving Daffin, his life had been one surprising thing after another. The sense of excitement at learning so many new things was beginning to grow. It was greater each day, as he learned not only about the world, but about himself.

"You have learned that you are descended from great Warriors, who have all bestowed upon you inherited gifts. These abilities that you have are new to you. You do not know how to employ them properly. You will. That is why we are here. The assemblage of talent is for your benefit. From Szavackka, you will learn what you need to learn about military life. He will teach you how to follow, as well as how to lead. He will also bring you closer to an understanding of your family heritage. You will learn the story of your most important ancestors, and the talents they pass down to you.

"Damanna, as you know is not here merely as housekeeper and governess to Delleyven. She will instruct you in everything else. I know of no person in the world as broadly read as she. Use your time with her well. You will never get a better chance to learn. The time of day you will be able to spend with her will fluctuate in order to accommodate the need to maintain her duties as governess. It may seem like a burden to be a secondary consideration to a child. It is one we must carry, for now.

"Beginning tomorrow morning, you will arrange times to receive instruction from Szavackka. A schedule of alternating days with he and Damanna will be set. Remember, the schedule of your instruction will flow around the demands of running the household smoothly. It would be preferable if no outside notice was taken of our presence here. It will be best if you stayed on the premises. No more walks into town. At least not alone."

"All the secrecy..." Gorrenn shook his head in dismay. "I'm not accustomed to it."

The Second Commander stood, and placed his fists on the desk, leaning forward. He stretched a bit and began pacing the room. "I have told you that there are people who would not like to know that the son of Harccosshan exists. The people I speak of are powerful people in the capitol, and in the Army of Eastern Malitok. If they knew you were here, we would have to flee far and fast to outrun them.

"The world you learned of as a boy is not the world of stark political reality that we all must live in. The government in Malitoka has become corrupt. Many who hold office there seek to further only their own aims, and those of their friends. Many people in towns like Ahngrist, and cities such as Partajann believe that the Accord

241

Councilors, and the Lector no longer care about the people and the land they govern."

"But, how can the people allow this?" Gorrenn was confused. His brow was deeply furrowed. He gazed at the floor, slowly shaking his head.

"The world, and Malitok are very large, as you know. Distances are great, much time is consumed in communicating. As a result, most change comes slowly. People expect this. When a change for the better is expected and does not come, people tend to believe it has just not come yet. People can hold expectations in abeyance for long periods of time. This is what poor governors count on, peoples' patience.

"The war in the East ended decades ago. No Giants live east of the Shield river. They were driven into the peninsular lleas and wiped out. Llea Tobarri was the last stronghold of the Giants in the East. Before that, it was

Llea Gavokki. The campaigns were long and devastating to the people of the East. They rightfully grew tired of having their sons, and yes, daughters lost to the wars. But they ended. Long ago.

"The Army of the East was never disbanded. It is true that a number of Cadres were shifted to the Western Army. This occurred after much reassignment of personnel had taken place. Warriors who had families in the East stayed. Many of the Cadres that joined the Western Army no longer exist because the men did not know each other, had no debt to their Cadre. The Warriors chose the Cadres they wished to join. Over time the debts were incurred. The brotherhood of the Cadres was reestablished. The Western Army lives and breathes its traditions in totality."

Massodice Parranck's face had brightened, for just a moment, as he spoke of the Western Army. His face, and tone, darkened again. "The Warriors who have remained in the East have forsaken their oaths of loyalty and honor. They serve government officers whose interests do not lie with the people. Voices of dissent are dealt with harshly. It is a situation no one saw coming. It represents a political evolution that is going in a direction that does harm to the people it is meant to serve.

"I fear that an entirely new thing is coming: War between men. Already, we have seen signs of it. The man we found on the grounds of Jenssal's home was sent from Malitoka. The evidence shows that he was on the grounds for only a short time. The only safe assumption is that he was not here alone."

Gorrenn could no longer look his Commander in the eye. He felt true shame at what he had just heard. He had never served alongside other Warriors. But he already felt brotherhood with them. His sense of disappointment and contempt rose within him. Anger was next. With it, the steel, and fire, and lightning sensation began to manifest itself. He deliberately distracted himself, thinking of food, horses, the drinking hall, anything. The sensation began to abate.

Parranck saw what Gorrenn was going through. He saw the frenzy rise within the young man, and subside. "Mastering it already?"

"What?" Gorrenn was clearly embarrassed by having shown so much emotion before his Commander.

"You controlled the rising of the frenzy just then. That's the beginning of mastery. Not all men can do it. Very few, actually, can master the frenzy. They are the special Warriors. Do not berate yourself for going through so much, right now. You are young. This is all very new to you. Give it time."

Parranck stopped his pacing and approached Gorrenn, placing a hand on his shoulder. "Gorrenn, you are the best. You are the hope of the future for some of us. As such, you are the terror that would keep other men from sleeping at night. Do not discount your worth to the world and its people. We are here. We few are here to help you begin the life that you were meant to live."

Gorrenn sat, mouth agape at what he had just heard. Szavackka entered with a tray of small sandwiches, and mugs of kaffe. "You have been working a long time, Massodice. Eat. Dinner comes late this evening. The young miss is performing music for her aunts and uncles."

The humdrum of home life was just what was needed to break the gloomy spell that had settled over the two men in the darkened room. Parranck took a chance on opening the drapes over the windows enough to admit the last of the afternoon daylight. The two men ate and drank silently. Gorrenn did not know what to say. The Second Commander felt that adding more to what he had said would break Gorrenn's spirit.

After a few minutes of the lingering silence between the two men, Parranck stood again. He resumed his position behind his desk. "Tomorrow, you will resume your training with Haditthue and Dobitto. Each day you will work in a different location. The two Warriors have instruction that if anyone is near, your training for the day will be passed over. Loss of a single day training will cost less than drawing attention. I hope this will be enough to keep interest in your activities constrained."

On his way through the house, Gorrenn heard the sound of the piano being played in the great room of the house. No doubt, is was Delleyven. In his room, Gorrenn found several books. From the broad range of subjects, he guessed Damanna had left them. Literature, art, mathematics, and science were all represented.

The science book intrigued him most of all. He began reading the chapter he found marked that explained what was known about family traits being passed from one generation to the next. He learned that the passing of intact ability from parent to child became known approximately one thousand years ago. It occurred, to some degree or another, in all families. The reason that the change in heritability had come was unknown. Warriors were not the only ones benefited this way. Farmers had long shown this ability in their bloodlines. Other traits became heritable over time. Warrior traits were among the last to arise in the scheme of transmissible ability.

The only trait group that took longer to arise was among the intellectually gifted. It had nonetheless arisen. Gorrenn knew that the city of Acquain hosted the greatest

minds in the world. It was referred to as the City of
Learning. Those who dwelt there were commonly called
'Learners.' He wondered how the inheriting of high
intelligence from one generation to the next would
ultimately work out. It seemed like a kind of conundrum.
He was learning about how far ahead of others he was. If
that held true for intellect, what was that like?

Lost in wondering, he was interrupted by a knock at
his door. It was Damanna. "I see you found the books I left
for you. Enjoying reading? The recital is finished. Dinner
will be served."

Gorrenn accepted the terse invitation for what it
was. Everyone was a little on edge. He was able to eat a
meal in the kitchen, watching Szavackka skillfully wrangle
the dishes. Jenssal and his family ate in the dining room
with Damanna. The balance of the evening was uneventful.
Gorrenn returned to his room, his reading, and sleep.

9

The gift of truth is the richest of all.

- The Song of Truth

The next morning, Gorrenn ate his breakfast, again in the kitchen with Szavackka. After eating, he pitched in cleaning dishes and sweeping up in the kitchen. While they worked, Szavackka began the first of their many instructional sessions.

"I was not sure whether to introduce you to your ancestors by starting with your father, Harccosshan, and working back, or not. After much thought on the subject, we will begin with your older ancestors and proceed forward in time to the present. The first of your ancestors to pass his abilities to his son was the Warrior, Jenrissal.

***

"Jenrissal was a Warrior that lived a thousand years ago. It was a dark time for men. There was nowhere in the world that men lived without fear of the Giants. Any town or village was subject to their depredation. Warriors lived among the other peoples of Malitok. Warriors were men dedicated to their warcraft. Over many centuries, they had become specialized, building families of their own. They brought together clans of family war fighters called cadres. Men who were true brethren fought better than other men. They protected each other with true ferocity.

251

Among the warriors, the ability to ride a horse skillfully in battle greatly enhanced fighting prowess. The best of them at riding was Jenrissal. Saying that he mastered the skill did an injustice to the oneness he achieved with his mount. He alone was able to ride with both hands free of the reins, employing his weapons. He considered his horse his brother. It bore him into battle after battle, fearlessly.

It was not until Jenrissal had sired a son that he experienced what we now know to be Warrior frenzy. In a battle with an aggressive troop of Giants, he felt a strange sense of detachment from his body. It suddenly became easier to swing his sword. His bow drew with barely any effort at all. He fired arrow after arrow, never missing his mark. With sword in one hand, and dagger in the other he waded into the center of the Giant attack. He struck and struck, and struck again. Standing over two of his fallen comrades, he fought off attack after attack, until help came.

Those with him said he fought like ten men that day. He was credited with turning the tide of a battle that surely would have been a bloody rout for the Warriors.

"After the battle, Jenrissal refused the praise heaped upon him by his peers. He continued to fight for many years. Each time, he lost his sense of self and became a devil to the Giants. It was he that was given credit for allowing the first of many areas to be considered 'free' of Giants. It was the town in the center of this area that later gained the name of 'City of Malitok': Malitoka, our capitol.

"In time his skill was sought by many towns and villages. His cadre moved from place to place in the east of Malitok, establishing the order of men. Centuries of war loomed ahead, for men. The seed of an idea, that an answer had been found, was planted in their minds. After many decades of war, Jenrissal passed away, leaving two generations of descendants who were master riders, and who experienced the frenzy. These are his ancestral gifts to all of his progeny, ultimately you. I understand that the Massodice reminded you that many strong family relationships exist within the Army. Before Jenrissal, no one had experienced Warrior frenzy. It stands to reason that since all Warriors now have that ability, that they are all somehow descended from him. With this understanding the brotherhood of Warriors takes on a deeper meaning for all men."

***

The afternoon brought a return of activities in the fields around Ahngrist. Gorrenn's appreciation for both Haditthue and Dobitto had been deepened by his morning lesson. Each in turn caught their young charge looking at them in a strange way, if only for an instant.

The skill drills of the afternoon seemed so much easier for Gorrenn. He was with his 'brothers.' Each new challenge, or suggestion was a wonder to him. It was happiness and true joy that motivated him now. He strove to outdo everything he was shown. Often, his exuberance led to hilarity. Being unfamiliar with things that he thought he should be able to do brought a predictable amount of failure to his efforts.

Dobitto concentrated his efforts on ensuring that Gorrenn became expert in fastening the leg straps for a military saddle. Small differences in adjustment meant the difference between having perfect control of the horse and not. Release from the straps, if needed, was as necessary to adjust for as anything else.

The next thing was going through the myriad nuanced details of a rider's rapport with the animal he was controlling. Refinement of a rider's ability to gain the confidence of a horse could make a huge difference in battle. Even more important, different horses were used in order to prove out Gorrenn's overall horsemanship. The practical side of this addressed the issue of a rider changing horses in the midst of a battle. Every horse a rider chose would need to instantly recognize the skill of its rider, and respond accordingly.

Haditthue had little difficulty getting Gorrenn up to fighting skill. It seemed to be in every sinew of his body. He gave no quarter in any fight. The two trained with blunted steel weapons. The weight and balance of the weapons were correct. The duels the two fought against each other were nightmares of flashing steel. Time after time, Haditthue bested Gorrenn only because of his experience.

Work with the bow went extremely well. Targets at varying distances were set up. Many different situations were posed for Gorrenn to deal with in hitting his mark. None were missed. Haditthue tried having Gorrenn run at full speed and fire arrows at targets the Dobitto was

dragging behind a war horse at full gallop. No misses.

Gorrenn felt as if he had been using the bow for his whole

life. He began to make smaller and smaller adjustments for

variations he detected in the shaft or fletching of different

arrows. As the afternoon wore on, he felt the bowstring

relax, just a tiny bit, due to his use of it, and the warming of

the sunlight.

To Gorrenn, the afternoon training session went by

very quickly. The trio returned to the house of Jenssal

before nightfall. Both Warriors were able to report that

Gorrenn's training was going well. Gorrenn again found a

new book in his room. It was a military guide to the

organization of the Western Army. In it was a graphic table

of the Troop Marks of various Cadres. A quick glance at it

before dinner revealed that the greatest number of Troop

Marks were tattoos. The branded Cadres were the ones

given the most arduous assignments. Gorrenn thought

257

Szavackka must be his most recent benefactor, since it was his responsibility to teach him about the Army.

After having his meal, again in the kitchen, Gorrenn spent the rest of the evening reading. He decided to go from book to book, a chapter at a time. He did not want to overlook anything in the books he had been given. More than just wanting to learn, the way he always had, he understood that he would be held accountable for his studies. He chose to seize the opportunity. He read late into the night.

10

If a man seeks to find truth, it will find him,

like a lion finding the hunter.

- The Song of Truth

The following morning, Gorrenn woke in his bed amid his books. Several had fallen to the floor in the night. This morning, he would be receiving instruction from Damanna, if the household schedule allowed for it. The idea stirred a new type of interest within him. He had not

259

experienced such an interest with regard to the lesson from Szavackka. He had so many questions to ask of her. The opportunity to learn from such a polymath was exciting.

The morning meal literally disappeared before he realized how fast he had eaten it. Cleaning up the dishes, he asked Szavackka if he had seen Damanna yet that morning. His answer was that she would meet with Gorrenn on the teradsh, after breakfast. Gorrenn began banging about the kitchen, hurrying in his attempt to finish cleaning up, helping Szavackka. The large cook was able to stand the frantic activity for only a few minutes before chasing Gorrenn from the room.

The Long Shadow morning was crisp and cool, the sunlight bright. Gorrenn had to wait a few minutes on the teradsh. As he was beginning to wonder if the lesson would be delayed, Damanna appeared. She was carrying a book with several page marks showing at the edges. Before

Gorrenn had a chance to ask a single question Damanna asked if Gorrenn had looked at any of the books she had left for him. She was suitably impressed that Gorrenn had managed a full chapter in each of the books.

Not missing a beat, Damanna launched into the lesson she had prepared for the morning. The subject was navigation. The reading of maps was discussed. Damanna spent a lot of time elucidating the method of sighting Darripont, the brightest star in the night sky. It is set in the heavens almost directly at perfect north. Using basic arithmetic, navigation based on its position is possible. Since it is not visible in the southern sky, other stars are employed in the same manner. As a first lesson, it turned out to be quite a full one. The duties of running the large household pressed upon Damanna. She was compelled to end the session before Gorrenn had a chance to ask questions of her.

The afternoon training session was very intense. Haditthue needed to ensure that Gorrenn would be as proficient as possible at unarmed combat. He brought padded gloves, and boot covers for both of them. Several instructional sparring sessions were held. To begin each session, Haditthue would explain the technique to be concentrated upon. Gorrenn responded by effectively employing the fighting technique. He literally had been born to it. As the intensity of the competition escalated, neither combatant could get an edge on the other. Gorrenn's speed, strength, and stamina were daunting, even to the Weapons Master of the Western Army. Haditthue suspected that as Gorrenn practiced more and more, the young man would very soon overcome his advantage of having more experience.

Dobitto felt left out for the most part and simply watched. When Haditthue had exhausted himself sparring, he began the riding instruction with Gorrenn. The balance of the training was concerned with the finer points of hands-free horsemanship. Dobitto decided that blind-riding would wait for another day. Using this two-man approach, the Warriors could expend as much energy training Gorrenn as possible. He never seemed to tire.

***

The next morning, Szavackka introduced another of Gorrenn's ancestors: Temmital. Born two centuries after Jenrissal, it was he who bestowed upon his descendants amazing skill with sword, dagger, and knife.

The wars against the Giants had continued unabated. As the population of mankind had expanded, so had the encroachment on land chiefly occupied by Giants. Temmital was a direct descendant of Jenrissal, and experienced Warrior frenzy as well. In this time, more and more Warriors were experiencing this because of familial, and clan association. The majority of Warriors still fought

263

without the frenzy, but its value in battle was not missed. As the military organization of the clan cadres became more formalized, leadership roles were bestowed upon the most accomplished Warriors. This meritocracy favored the Warriors who experienced the frenzy in battle.

Jenrissal's skill in riding was passed on to his descendants as well as the frenzy. Warriors had adopted the use of horses in battle with their much larger enemy as a way of trying to balance the scales. A Warrior on horseback weighed nearly as much as a Giant. At a full gallop, the riding pair could overrun a single Giant, although the impact could be devastating for any, or all, of the three.

The most effective use of the horse was in employing its speed against the Giants. The Giants were larger and significantly slower than a man. The horse allowed for attack from many different angles in a short period of time. The tried and tested method of bringing down one of the monsters was applying an overwhelming number of wounds. The use of horses vastly increased the effectiveness of this strategy.

The broadsword was the main weapon used in confrontational combat against the Giants. The grotesque creatures often seemed to shrug off scores of arrow strikes. The sword was employed to deliver more devastating wounds. Half as long as a man's height, the length of it allowed the

Warrior to strike from outside the reach of an unarmed giant. The broadsword was a prized possession of a Warrior, always passed down from father to son. A Warrior who entered the service of a cadre without an inherited broadsword was awarded one in recognition of his membership in the brotherhood of Warriors. Unbloodied swords usually found themselves early into battle. This was intended to prove the sword, as well as its master.

The dagger and knife had existed even longer than the sword. Born of essential tools, all men carried them. Most women carried knives as well. Being brought into use in warfare was a natural outgrowth of their use in everyday life. In this time of military development, knives were employed as recognition of rank. Blade shapes and length varied with the increasing order of rank achieved. Hilt markings were identifiers of clan cadres.

The dagger evolved from the knife into a purposeful weapon. In a world where there were Giants to be feared, it was inconceivable to go about without one. Since it was such a broadly familiar weapon, standardization had not come to its general manufacture. Lengths varied up to three quarters of the length of a sword. Blade width, and thickness, depended more on the mood of the maker and the availability of materials than anything else.

266

Temmital had become the prohibitive master of all uses of these weapons in warfare. In the early days of his life as a Warrior, his mastery made itself evident. No man could stand against him in training duels. The outcome was always the same: Temmital overcame his opponent in short order. In battle against the Giants, his value in being able to strike accurately, while dodging the blows of the monsters was great. Many Warriors found themselves losing ground in battles with Giants, only to have Temmital intercede and turn the tide of battle.

Temmital was famous for being the only Warrior to stand between two giants attacking him and successfully fight them off until other members of his cadre came to his aid. So reliable was his ability in battle, the other members of his cadre called his sword Darripont, after the prime navigation star. To them, it could always be counted upon in battle, like the star was relied upon in finding your way in strange lands.

Temmital took this sort of recognition in stride. His commitment to his life as a Warrior led him to believe that the most important quality of his skill was that he ought to share it with his brothers-in-arms. This is the origin of Weapons Masters for the Armies. From this time forward, the organized bands of clan cadres selected the most skilled among them. These Warriors the bore the responsibility of ensuring that every Warrior had equal knowledge of fighting skills and techniques.

11

Truth, kept closed, and hidden,

is harm to the keeper, and to all.

- The Song of Truth

The daily routine of morning instruction followed by afternoon field work had begun to rest very easy with Gorrenn. So it was, to his surprise the next morning, when Haditthue roused him from sleep before dawn. He tossed a field pack at Gorrenn's feet. "We work this morning to improve your skills." This was all he said before turning and leaving the room. Along with his surprise at the change in schedule, Gorrenn was aware that his second cousin had entered his room without awakening him. Stealth was obviously part of a Warriors training.

Gorrenn met up with Haditthue and Dobitto in the barn behind Jenssal's house. Dobitto had fed the animals, but each had to saddle their own mount. The horse that Gorrenn had been riding for the last few days was not among the trio selected. Dobitto pointed out to Gorrenn that the horse he was to ride would be his from now on.

The horse was named Tuzhandek. It was known to be particularly spirited. Gorrenn was warned to proceed carefully, but firmly with the animal. It was as important to have the horse trust you as it was for him to understand that all commands given were to be followed without hesitation.

Beginning from this moment, the bond between horse and Warrior would be formed.

The ride out, to the area in which they would work that morning, was through fog. Each man ate from a meat and bread roll that had been prepared last night. The field packs included water jugs as well. Gorrenn understood that there were probably multiple reasons for changing their schedule. The field work each afternoon was eventually going to be discovered. This change forestalled that eventuality. The change was also necessary to assess Gorrenn's performance in varying conditions. Lastly, it gave the household a change in routine. One more opportunity to avoid the discovery that a group of Warriors were operating in a peaceful town like Ahngrist.

Tuzhandek turned out to be an obviously superior specimen. He was a hand taller than most fighting horses. Gorrenn felt him responding to small cues from his legs even while riding out to the working area. He suspected he had been trained well. If it were possible to form an actual friendship with a horse, this might be the animal for it. Gorrenn's study of Warrior ways revealed much about the bond between a horse and the Warrior who rode it. The two depended so heavily upon each other that a near-symbiosis formed. A Warrior would always make certain that his mount was watered, fed and cared for before tending to his own needs.

The morning's training centered around familiarizing Gorrenn with the finer points of hands-free horsemanship. Doing so with Tuzhandek was a step to building the bond between them. Haditthue's weapons instruction focused on techniques of fighting from horseback, the essential battle strength of a Cadre. Drill after drill was run, deepening the learning relationship between Gorrenn and his horse. The culmination of the morning exercise was a full-gallop attack drill. With the horse at full speed beneath him, Gorrenn began to feel the exhilaration of battle that led to Warrior's frenzy. The sense of near invulnerability that enveloped him was new and terribly exciting. Gorrenn had to concentrate to avoid losing himself to it completely.

***

The afternoon instructional session turned out to be another with Szavackka. The kitchen turned out to be a quiet place in the afternoons. It was a good place to sit together and learn. The lesson today was to be about two of Gorrenn's ancestors. The first was Malissoran. He was Gorrenn's great, great, great grandfather. Living one hundred twenty years ago, he changed Warrior ways for the better with his absolute mastery of the use of the long bow and the lance.

History suggested that Malissoran excelled with bow and lance as a compensation for being shorter in

273

stature than his fellow Warriors. He was gifted with horse riding skills second to none. He was master of drawn weapons. He added complete mastery of archery and lance-work to his arsenal of fighting skills. His reach may have been shorter with the sword, but he could kill at distance better than any other Warrior. His use of the bow was so thoroughly different that several redesigns of the ancient weapon evolved during his lifetime.

In his lifetime, Malissoran saw the Warrior's bow become heavier, longer, and more powerful. New, more aerodynamic, and yet heavier arrows evolved as well. A war arrow propelled by a Warriors bow could penetrate a five-inch tree trunk. Such power was essential in making the bow useful in war against the Giants.

The developments in bow technology were a sea-change in the wars against the Giants. More and more areas of Malitok were cleared of their presence, and at a faster rate. This was fortuitous as it coincided with a surge in the rate of human population growth. The potential for change in many things had accumulated for many centuries. It was now coming to fruition.

Small bits of skill and intelligence were passed from parent to child in Malitokan Warrior families. Other disciplines of life benefited in like manner. Farmers, miners, carpenters and builders; men and women working in many different areas of human endeavor were beginning to see their children carry their talents into the future.

Malissoran contributed much to developments in bow warfare. Likewise, he added to the advancement in the use of the fighting lance. As an outgrowth of Malissoran's skill, many different types of war lance came into being. A long, lightweight lance was developed for use on horseback. Easily maneuvered from the saddle, it had an iron tip as long as a man's forearm. Many Giants were felled by Warriors at full gallop on horseback, wielding this frightening weapon. Throwing lances were developed that a Warrior could hurl over long distances. Heavy lances, that Warriors could stand in ranks and face massed charges of the beast-like enemy, were invented.

Gorrenn's great grandfather was the last of his ancestors he learned about. Ikallotan was a Warrior who had fought in the time of driving the last of the Giant hordes west of the Shield River. Reporting the history this way was a device of the historians. The truth was simply that the last of the Giants east of the Shield River were killed. At its narrowest point, the Shield River is two passukhs wide. The Giants never developed boat-building skills.

Ikallotan's contribution to Gorrenn's existence was strength and stamina well beyond that of other men. Gorrenn was at last able to personally relate to an ancestor because he himself had not yet lived a single day in which he had become tired. Work and war training were the same to him. Others always brought things to a halt because their day was done. Gorrenn had lived and worked like this for a long time before he realized that he was different from other men. He had always kept it to himself. It never seemed to be anything worthy of conversation.

Ikallotan was able to engage Giants in battle for such lengths of time that it was often the fall of night that led to the conclusion of a battle. Many Giants had fallen because they simply exhausted themselves battling with Ikallotan. Many more had fallen because they could not see him striking at them in the near dark of night. His sword, dagger and lance all did their work in the gloaming of day with the same ferocity they had at dawn. Arrows by the score flew from his bow. The armorers for his Cadre worked extra duty keeping him supplied with sufficient numbers of arrows.

The afternoon lesson came to a close with Szavackka advising Gorrenn, "Tomorrow, we speak of your most recent ancestor, your father, Harccosshan." He began his clattering about the kitchen, preparing meals for the evening.

Gorrenn shuttered his excitement at the news that he would at last be learning about his father. He left the kitchen to Szavackka. He decided to take advantage of the change in schedule to familiarize himself a little more completely with the afternoon routines of the household. Reading on the teradsh was the easiest way to "see without being seen."

He watched the men going about their gardening. It really impressed him how the men could appear to be so diligently gardening, and yet nothing changed. No flowers were cut, none of the trees or shrubs were pruned. Frankly they did not need any such attention. The grounds were already so immaculately kept that the work of the men in the garden was almost perfectly wasted. A weed was plucked from the planting beds here and there. Loose leaves were picked up. The men each had a small basket into which they put garden debris. Gorrenn suspected that each basket held a weapon of some sort or another. He also counted on the men to be carrying weapons on their persons.

As the afternoon wore on towards the evening, Damanna and Delleyven strolled by, engaged in some instructional lesson or other. The pair had been walking through the garden, a continuous commentary being exchanged between them. They paused briefly, and Damanna bid Delleyven go into the house and wait for her. She approached Gorrenn, sitting on the edge of the teradsh.

"Lovely afternoon for spying. If you are going to observe others, you have to be more believable. Turn a page in your book every once in a while." After the briefest

of winks, she was off to the house, and her young charge.

Gorrenn was as impressed as ever with the formidable

governess.

12

Truth can heal the heart,

or shatter the world.

- The Song of Truth

The evening meal came and went uneventfully.
Gorrenn made ready for the next day by burying himself in
his books Hour by hour, he read as much as he could in
each book, trying to give each an equal share of his time.
The hour grew late, and as he made ready to douse the light

in his room and sleep, he heard noise in the hall. Unusual for the hour, Gorrenn went to the door to investigate. Just as he reached the doorknob to open it, a knock from the other side surprised him.

Standing in the hallway was Szavackka, dressed as Gorrenn had never seen him, in dark clothing, boots and a dark broad-brimmed hat. "Make a bedroll, pack what you need. We are leaving. Now. Quietly. We do not want to waken the rest of the house." He turned away from the door without waiting for a response. The calm certainty in his voice carried the weight of orders relayed from higher authority. Szavackka worked his way down the hallway stopping at each door to instruct each member of Parranck's team who slept on the same floor as Gorrenn.

Gorrenn quickly assembled his bedroll. He gathered his few belongings. He took one last, brief look at the room to ensure he was leaving nothing behind. He darkened the room. Gorrenn left the room where his life as a Warrior, son of the ultimate Warrior had begun. He walked through the house. Every room seemed to have some activity in it. Lights were being extinguished in rooms as people left them. No one was moving slowly.

The main floor of the house was quiet. Jenssal, and his daughter's rooms were in another wing of the large house. Damanna's room was there also. That part of the house slept, undisturbed by the hushed activity of the men who served Massodice Parranck.

Gorrenn followed one of the men to the barn behind the great house. Inside, he found teams of horses being hitched to two wagons. Each of the wagons was being loaded. Half of what was put into the wagons appeared to be weapons of every description. Swords, daggers, knives were tightly bundled, padded to keep from rattling against each other. Bows and quivers of arrows were stacked and stored for a journey. War lances, mostly of the throwing variety, lined the floor of each wagon.

As he progressed through the barn, he saw Warriors saddling their mounts. The way the men were dressed, it would be hard to mistake them for anything but Warriors, now that Gorrenn knew what he was looking at. He made for Tuzhandek, and began saddling him. He was about to ask about leg straps for the journey when he saw a Warrior fitting his to the saddle on his horse. "Always be ready." The words echoed through Gorrenn's mind as he made ready for riding in the manner of Warriors.

Gorrenn had noticed a separate pack lain at the feet of each mount. There was one next to Tuzhandek. After satisfying himself that his saddle was perfectly ready for riding, Gorrenn picked up the pack from the floor of the barn. It was heavy in his hands. He looked up to see Haditthue standing before him. "Light weapons pack. Short sword, dagger, six knives. This is your pack. Secure it to your saddle. When you are finished, come to the back of the barn. The Massodice wants to speak with you." He turned and left.

Securing the weapons pack to his horse's saddle as quickly as he could, Gorrenn walked to the back of the barn. Massodice Parranck was there, stowing maps in a trunk to be put in the first wagon. The trunk was marked with his legend, two crossed arrows penetrating a star. It appeared as though hours of work preparing for the departure had already been done.

The Second Commander of the Western Army looked up from his task and smiled at Gorrenn. "Your life as a Warrior begins in earnest. Your first mission is to accompany our small troop, as we leave Ahngrist."

Gorrenn felt himself straighten a bit as he stood before his commander. Noticing this, the Massodice put his hand on Gorrenn's shoulder. "For now, acting un-military is what is needed. Relax. You might have noticed a lack of saluting while we were in the house of Jenssal. This has all been necessary in order to accomplish what we have here."

He saw the confusion in Gorrenn's eyes. "It is very unusual for a commander to explain himself, but this is a very unusual circumstance. We have accomplished only part of what we set out to do with you, here, in Ahngrist. The man who was discovered on the grounds of Jenssal's house, finally shared his secrets with the man you know as Katosse. Yes, he is part of this team. He does a great many different things in aid of the Western Army. Managing a livery stable is just one of them.

"The man found here was sent to spy on us by men in the east of Malitok whose goals are different from those of a great many people. These men create laws to serve themselves at the expense of others. They enforce their laws with the power of the Eastern Army. As corrupt as it may have become, it is still borne up by the might of Warriors. His presence here means that the powerful men in the east know we are here. It is almost certain that they do not know why we are here and what we have been doing. We can take no chances with this situation.

"I hoped we would be able to complete your introduction to the life of a Warrior. We have not. The balance of your training, minus the benefit of Damanna's teaching will be on the road to our next destination. Damanna will remain here to safeguard Jenssal's family."

Gorrenn's mouth hung open. He understood only part of what the Massodice had just said. "Safeguard?" The word escaped his mouth before he could control himself.

"You did not work it out? Excellent. Her presence here seems much more secure. If you did not discover her Warrior status, I doubt anyone else will. In addition to her mountainous wealth of knowledge, Damanna is a Warrior of no mean description. I would fight beside her anywhere, as I would with any member of this team."

Gorrenn thought for a moment that the Massodice had just paid him a compliment, but quickly buried the thought of it, inwardly embarrassed. He involuntarily looked down toward the floor of the barn. In what Gorrenn thought was an extremely unusual show of personal connection and emotion, the Massodice put his fist under the chin of the young Warrior, and brought Gorrenn's gaze up to his own.

"You will be part of this team, very soon, Gorrenn. You are Harccofenti, Little Arrow. That is your name for now. What name you earn remains to be seen. Go, we ride very soon."

Gorrenn walked back to Tuzhandek. Once there, he saw the Warrior he knew as Meddace re-strapping the weapons pack to his saddle. Before he could speak to question, Meddace explained, "You were too hasty in strapping. See? Like so. Now it won't slip off if things get rough."

"Thank you. There are many such things I still need to learn."

The party completed its preparations, and the Warriors began to mount their horses. Gorrenn asked Meddace, "Any idea where we are going?"

Without looking up from his last bit of saddle adjusting, Meddace answered, "Only one place for us to go. Estox. Home."

Gorrenn knew it from his reading as a boy. Estox, also called Nyugati Tenger, 'Home of the Warrior.' It was the one city in the entire western half of Malitok where Warriors lived. The people of Malitok considered Warriors to be so violent that they were unwelcome in settled cities and towns not on the frontier.

Few outsiders had ever ventured to go to Estox. Little was known of it other than it was not like other cities. Where other towns and cities clustered people and buildings together, the plan of Estox was chiefly concerned with keeping space between its residents. As a result, the city of Estox spread over many passukhs.

The other thing that Gorrenn knew about Estox was that it lay many passukhs on the far side of the Shield River. River crossings were not taken lightly by anyone. The mighty Shield River was the glacial and pluvial drain for two-thirds of the continent. It was said that not one drop of water existed in the world that had not flowed down the Shield River. Terminating in the Affoon Delta it emptied into the great inland sea Malitok Torrotta.

The small 'cadre' began its quiet, easy ride out of Ahngrist. Each of the wagons took a separate route to the western edge of town, where they were to again form a group. In similar fashion, pairs of riders took different paths through town.

Every member of the team was highly sensitized to the slightest hint of observation, or that anyone was showing more than the most casual interest in them. After a short while the reformed group left the town proper and rode west. There were two riders in the lead of the group, two outriders on either side, and two trailing riders. In the dark of night, the concession to security gave way to traveling in an obvious military formation.

Gorrenn had thought his life had changed drastically after leaving Daffin. With the things Parranck had told him, he knew the truly serious changes in his life lay ahead of him.

All truths cannot be known.

Mystery will persist beyond all discovery.

- The Song of Truth

Part Three

1

Giving is life done unto itself.

- The Song of Giving

The overnight beginning of the journey to Estox was an inauspicious start to an important part of Gorrenn's life. He gained a better understanding of why persistent readiness was a by-word of the Army. The group of men had roused from their beds, saddled their horses, packed the wagons and left the house of Jenssal in less than an hour. The passage through Ahngrist had been accomplished

293

without rousing the citizens of the town from their sleep. The wagons had previously been prepared for such an eventuality by greasing the axles, and ensuring that every possible sound was suppressed.

He learned much about organizing a night patrol formation. The outrider position, that he was in, gave him an important, if secondary, role in the movement of the group. In the night's journey through the countryside west of Ahngrist, he became familiar with the trust a rider has for his horse. It was the longest period of time he had been on horseback. More and more, as the night wore on, Tuzhandek felt as though he was becoming a part of him. After a long while, the horse simply held his position in the patrol formation without prompting from Gorrenn.

The formation of the traveling party was organized in Malitokan military fashion. A single scout rode ahead of the troop just out of sight. Two lead riders rode at the head of the main group. The wagons were separated by riders leading unmounted horses whose riders rested in the wagons. A pair of generally unassigned riders rode here as well. The Massodice rode in the center of the formation. Two outriders covered positions on either side of the group. In this fashion, eyes and ears covered every angle from which a threat might appear.

The group, which had reformed outside of town, now rode through the hills west of Ahngrist. Soon they would turn northwestward toward the Ka'Apatta Mountains. The night had become quite cold. It was now Esirren, the second month of Long Shadow, and killing frosts were a real threat. Gorrenn did not have winter clothes. He made do with his coat and hat pulled close around him. He would have to find heavier clothing for the coming months of colder weather. He did not know how this would be done, since the group with Massodice

Parranck had been ordered to move so suddenly and surreptitiously.

The Warriors with the group had taken turns resting in the back of the wagons. Gorrenn had refused such relief. He did not feel the need for rest. He understood more of why this was so, after his sessions with Szavackka introduced him to his ancestor, Ikallotan. He knew he would well be able to finish another entire day's ride before needing sleep.

His senses were heightened by the new experiences that he was having. He looked as far ahead as he could, his eyes having long ago adjusted to seeing by only starlight. The moons had set before they left Ahngrist, and as soon as they entered the forest west of town the darkness had enveloped the group completely. Showing no light as they moved through the open country was a very familiar technique employed by the Army. Gorrenn was grateful for having Tuzhandek's eyes to help him.

As the dawn approached, three Warriors came to Gorrenn's position on the right of the group. One of them was Meddace. The other two, Gorrenn recognized from the garden at Jenssal's house. The right-side outriders were to be relieved. Since Gorrenn had refused an opportunity to rest, he would accompany Meddace in the scout position, and learn from him as the morning's journey progressed. His training would continue at every opportunity that presented itself.

The topography of the land became steeper. The small military band was now in the foothills of the Ka'Apatta Mountains. At dawn, Szavackka distributed food packs and water jugs to every rider. Massodice Parranck gave the order that no game was to be taken until they were in the mountains themselves. The morning meal was eaten while the group continued to put distance between itself and Ahngrist.

Meddace was prolific in trying to teach Gorrenn everything he could about manning the position of column scout rider. So much depended on the skill of the Warrior assigned to the task, that experienced Warriors were usually selected. Where, when, and how to look, and what specifically to look for were covered. Using the angle of sunlight to your advantage, and moving so the sun angle helped instead of hindered you, was emphasized. Describing how this was all different in cloudy, rainy, or foggy weather conditions, was included in the instruction. Meddace tried to ensure that if this was the only lesson in riding scout position that Gorrenn ever received, it would be enough.

For his part, Gorrenn paid strict attention to every word Meddace said. He had begun to sense the urgency behind the words of the Massodice. The sudden departure from Ahngrist only made this seem all the more serious. The weight of things that Gorrenn did not know, had begun to press down on his life. Even though he in no way felt inadequate, it was still all very new to him. The steps he was taking, in leaving his life as a farmer, and becoming something entirely unexpected, were becoming increasingly larger. Each new level of experience seemed to carry a multiple of the risk, and worry, of the preceding one.

The small troop came at last to a place where the road diverged into two separate paths; one to the west, and one to the northwest. Turning to the right, the group made for the pass between northern and southern Ka'Apatta Mountains. Beyond that lay Quolluta Jatt, the departure point for crossing the mighty Shield river. While in the mountains proper, the scout would ride farther ahead, and need to cover much more ground, assuring safety for the group. Gorrenn and Meddace were relieved at mid-day, when a brief rest for the animals allowed for a small, somewhat communal meal for the Warriors.

The terrain steepened, and the pace of the group's progress slowed. The Massodice asked for Gorrenn to join him at the center of the formation. The afternoon's travel would be an opportunity for the Second Commander to educate his young charge in earnest. The number of things that needed to be discussed was enormous. Having to do so, under these conditions, was very much not what the Massodice wanted, but it was what was going to happen.

As they talked, the afternoon sun bore down on their hats and the front of their jackets. In the cool Long Shadow air, it warmed them. Parranck decided to adopt an easy tone for what he had to say to the new recruit. "You cannot forget that men have fought for centuries, carving out an existence for themselves in a hostile environment.

This has made men different from what they might have been without the need to destroy the Giants. Men have never lived without the presence of the Giants as the very bane of their existence."

The Massodice went on to speak of many things that afternoon. He explained that leadership of men involved learning everything you could, about as many different things as possible. A leader never knew which information would be the essential thing, to win a campaign, or save lives. In this way, a leader comes to understand that everything is important. A person who strove to lead others had to have their interests at heart. The heaviest weight of leadership is having the interests of your command at heart, and having to send your command into battle. Somehow it always seemed to have a self-destructive quality to it. The way of war was difficult. The discussion of the necessities of leadership philosophy filled the balance of the afternoon ride into the mountains.

Camp was made for the night at the foot of the first long climb into Ka'Apatta Pass. The pass itself spanned a distance of over ten passukhs. Steep mountainside sat on either side of the pass. The road switched back many times before getting to the first decline. It would be scouted thoroughly, before the main group of men set foot upon it. Haditthue and Meddace were given the assignment. The scouting foray would take several hours.

The camp was set so that it could be struck and left at a moment's notice. Only the barest necessities were removed from the wagons. For the night ahead, the horses would remain in partial tack, so they could be quickly saddled, if need be. The horses were watered and fed, ahead of the men.

A single fire was lit for preparation of a hot meal. Szavackka quickly set a hearty, filling meal of meats and bread for the men. The sentry assignments were set. The men in camp remained largely quiet. Little talk passed between them. The closeness of the mountain walls around them was a stark change from the openness of the plains, and made them uncomfortable. The sounds of the wind coursing through the mountain pass rose and fell in an uneven rhythm. The horses were uneasy. The sleep that came to the men was a restless one.

Before the dawn lightened the eastern sky, the camp was struck and the small band began the trek through Ka'Apatta Pass. The name evoked the memory of an important battle against the Giants. It had been through this very pass that the last of the Giants east of the Shield River had been pursued before their destruction. The dark of night clung to the steep canyon walls. Long after dawn, it was only the lightening of the sky directly overhead that provided illumination. The cold air of night remained long into the morning.

The Time of Long Shadows

Haditthue and Meddace had returned before the small band had decamped. Their scouting mission had revealed no one ahead of them in the confines of the pass. The two Warriors now rested in one of the wagons. Although an effort was made to move quietly, every step of every hoof echoed back off the walls of the steep, narrow defile. The outriders were confined to the roadway, and positioned themselves ahead of and behind the wagons. Speed on the switchback road was not possible. Progress was made at only a slow, moderate pace.

The shadow of the eastern ridge was half way down the western side of Ka'Apatta Pass when the last switchback turn was made. The outriders returned to their positions astride the roadway. The party's pace quickened. The last decline was made down to the small plain that terminated at Quolluta Jatt. The plain was some ten passukhs wide and twelve or so long. It was informally referred to as the Ka'Apatta Plain. The road before them was open.

2

The act of giving enriches the giver.

- The Song of Giving

The name of Ka'Apatta Pass literally means 'Capture Pass' in the old language of Malitok. It was given because it is near the place where a Giant was captured for the first time. Prior to this event, for more than a thousand years, only mutual killing had taken place between men and Giants. The giants fought like beasts, with every ounce of strength they had. Hour after hour, they would battle against men until they dropped dead from exhaustion, or were slain.

The battle of Ka'Apatta Pass took place two hundred years earlier. The preparation for this sort of organized campaign had taken may years. The family and clan cadres had been organized into formal Cadres of the Army. This process had occupied decades. Many personal accommodations that existed in family-based groups had to be dealt with. Individual merit would supersede familial bonds. Henceforth the Army would exist in its own right, supported by a fledgling government in Malitoka, the city chosen as capitol.

The last of the Giants that dwelt on the eastern side of the Shield River had been beaten back, and pursued onto the plain west of the mountain pass. The maneuver that forced them into the pass in the first place, had been costly for the Cadres that engaged them. Many hundreds of Warrior lives were lost in assuring that all of the Giants were funneled into the mountain pass. Long before the pursuit had begun, Cadres had been positioned in the hills on either side of the plain west of the pass. The strategy had been to force them into an area from which they could not escape. After centuries of warfare against the direst of enemies, men would have half the world safe from their depredation.

The battle that took place on the plain west of Ka'Apatta Pass was not spoken of. No grand heroic ballads were ever written. The deeds done were memorable only for their ferocity and finality. On one hand, the view of history might ultimately be that Ka'Apatta Pass was simply a slaughter, little else. Once the Giants were herded onto the plain, wave after wave of Warrior attacks began. Having no place to go, the Giants fought back with monstrous savagery. Though not entirely an unknown

308

thing, Giant females participated in the battle. With the added impetus of protecting their young, they were merciless in fighting. 'Tooth and nail' were the least of the extent thrown into the battle that day.

By the end of the day, only a small band of Giant males, and a few young remained on the field. All of the Cadres had been thrown into the fight, and sustained enormous casualty counts. The Cadres posted on the hillsides were tested over and over by Giants seeking to find a way out of the maelstrom of gore on the small plain at Ka'Apatta.

Time had to be taken to reorganize for continued attacks until the Giants were gone. During this time, in the evening of the day of battle, a sound arose from the band of Giants remaining. Starting as a very low susurration, it rose in volume until it echoed across the plain to the hillsides. This was the song of the Giants. Very low in pitch, slow and rhythmical, it continued uninterrupted for more than two hours.

Only spoken of by men in hushed tones, Giant song was considered by most men to be a legend. No one had ever heard the sound at close proximity. Drifting down mountain valleys, or across vast distances on the plains, it was carried on the wind, and considered to be part of it. Now, here, without question, the Giants were singing. Men could not understand any of its importance to the Giants. The sound, the song, ended abruptly. The Giants that remained stood their ground, waiting.

The last of the attacks began. Within an hour, only one lone Giant remained standing. All of the others around him had been slain. Young, old, males and females were all dead. He began advancing on the Warrior Cadre that he faced. A plan to capture the monster, if possible, was put into action. Ropes as thick as a man's arm were drawn around the Giant by horses. Wound in carefully planned loops, they first bound the monster's ankles and legs. With only a crude club in his enormous hands, the Giant could only flail at the ropes around him. Slowly, more ropes were brought to loop higher and higher on the Giant's body until he was immobilized. Bellowing and straining against the ropes, he was drawn onto a sledge, and taken to a special stockade that had been built for the purpose of confining the Giant in order that he might be studied.

Once within the stockade, the ropes were loosened and the Giant allowed to work himself free of his constraints. For hours he raged and bellowed, assaulting the tree-trunk walls of his confinement. Time and time again, he threw his enormous body against the walls, shaking them mightily. Ultimately, the beast exhausted himself, and stopped. After regaining his strength, the Giant began again slamming himself into the walls of his cell, hoping to breach them. This cycle of assault, and rest period, went on for three days.

When at last, the Giant desisted in trying to escape from his confinement, he sat in the center of the cell and began the Giant song heard days earlier on the battlefield. The low susurration rose and fell. The Giant periodically paused to listen for an answering song. None was to be heard. Hour after hour, he sang and listened. Hour after hour, his song diminished in volume until it could hardly be heard at all.

Finally, the only sign that the song continued was the rhythmic rise and fall of the Giant's chest. When at last even that was no longer evident, his captors called out to him, hoping to rouse him from sleep. They received no response. A long pole was brought to prod the monster and wake him. The first touch of it brought no response. The second prodding, more forceful, toppled the Giant over onto his side, revealing him to be dead.

***

The small military group traversed the Ka'Apatta plain without incident. The decision had been made that when the party was in sight of Quolluta Jatt, the military formation would be abandoned. They would arrive in the river-crossing town as any other group would, together, but without the tell-tale military behavior. The Massodice had emphasized that all saluting and recognition of rank were to be absent while undertaking the river crossing.

Massodice Parranck had been careful to point out to Gorrenn, that an extra measure of care was to be taken while in this town, and during the crossing of the river. Quolluta Jatt was a place where men who could do no other work came to eke out an existence. With no other prospects for earning a living, men became utterly deceitful and untrustworthy. It would be best to consider everyone he might encounter in the little town to be a thief.

The Shield River was a raging, unforgiving torrent at the calmest of times, and could become much worse in no time at all. Men died here, working on the river boats. Death was at hand at all times on the river. It was a fact of life for the men who worked the boats. Men died, and that was it. Few funerals were ever held. There seemed to be an endless supply of men ready to fill the empty spots on crew rosters.

At least one boat was lost each year. Unfortunately, this was the time of year when boats were lost. The necessity of the crossing was undeniable. Massodice Parranck had made the decision to move Gorrenn, and continue his introduction to the Army, to the west. The west side of the river held fewer risks of discovery and interference. The crossing would have to be made as soon as it could be. The crossing would be arranged by Haditthue.

As the group entered Quolluta Jatt, the most notable thing was that no one took any notice of them at all. At least that's how it seemed. To Massodice Parranck, no such lack of notice was likely, or even possible. Getting through, and out of, this sleazy mess of a town, as quickly as possible, was his main objective. As far as he was concerned, every door and window hid eyes that were taking the measure of their group as they passed.

They had to traverse the entirety of the main street in town in order to get to the boat docks. Each building facade was a study in dilapidation. Applying a coat of paint was a one-time event in Quolluta Jatt, never to be repeated. Repairs, where they were visible, were haphazard at best. Dark, dirty, and dingy, the entire town reeked of fish, river water, and offal. If there were a competition in this town to be the worst, most run-down looking building, Gorrenn would not be surprised. He also would not be able to choose a winner.

Every other building was occupied by a drinking hall of one kind or another. They all were in operation. Music and the now-familiar drinking hall stench flowed from the open doorways of each one. Gorrenn wondered how so many establishments that competed with each other could remain in business in such a small town. He guessed that the constant flow of people crossing the river kept them supplied with customers.

They stopped at what seemed to be an office for one of the boat operators. The Warriors dismounted, but remained with their horses. The dark, unwashed squalor of the place began to make itself more evident with each minute that passed waiting for Haditthue to return from negotiating the fee for their passage. Looking around,

Gorrenn observed that no care at all was ever given to the appearance of any of the buildings.

Haditthue returned and reported to Massodice Parranck that the boat operator said it was too late in the day to launch. Launching a boat now would mean that the return tow up the river would have to be conducted at sunset, very dangerous for the crew. They would have to wait for the morning to cross the river. The Second Commander pulled a pouch of gold coins from his belt and sent Haditthue back to see if it was in fact too late after all.

On his second return from the boat operator's office, Haditthue reported, grinning from ear to ear, that the danger of a late crossing was manageable after all. They would embark immediately.

3

Free, and cheerful giving

is the light of the sun,

ridding lives of darkness.

- The Song of Giving

The dock at the river was old, but in good repair.
Gorrenn took note of this difference from the condition of
the rest of the town immediately. All of the visible
equipment was arranged neatly, so as not to interfere with

work done on the dock itself. Ropes and tackle of every sort were available for immediate use in landing and loading the riverboat. A tall, counter-balanced crane stood astride the entire dock. Its swing would allow loading of boats on either side of the dock. A stack of balance-weight stones rested on its own pedestal which penetrated the dock, and rested directly on the river bed. The size of the stack of stones demonstrated that the capacity of the crane was great. As their group approached the dock, men were rigging several of the stones in a rope netting sling.

Even taller than the crane, was a tower that stood next to the dock. The top of the tower held a small enclosed position for a signalman. Gorrenn could see that with the afternoon's clear, sunny sky, that the signalman was using a mirror signaling device. Gorrenn knew that the device was called a heliostat.

The signal was being sent to their destination on the river, Medvazhikki Landing. This was where they would leave the boat, and continue their journey to Estox. He wondered what device might be used for signaling in cloudy, or rainy weather. Some discoveries would have to wait for more opportune times. Now was the time for keeping to oneself, not being overtly curious, as he was, about everything.

In even more stark contrast to the run-down condition of the town of Quolluta Jatt, the riverboat 'Dragon' sat proudly at the side of the river dock. Freshly painted, it shown brightly against the drab surroundings. Its appearance left no doubt as to why the town was here in the first place. Trimmed in bright red, the white gunwales stood out. The stained deck, the two masts, and bowsprit were clean as they could be. The rigging was so neat, it was hard to think of the boat as a working craft. The yards and spars were lined up in parallel with each other. There was not one piece of rigging or line out of place.

The small group of Warriors, dressed as they were in common clothes moved down the dock toward the boat. They were met at mid-point by the first mate of the Dragon, who gave his name as Livey. He asked them to wait while the boat was readied for passage. A whistle sounded on the deck of the boat and men appeared from everywhere. Deck hatches flew open, and doors were thrown back. The deck of the boat literally came to life with the sudden activity of the crewmen.

One of the crew ran to the bow of the boat and began to fly a chefiti. Not unlike the chefitis Gorrenn had flown on the plains as a farm boy, it rose quickly in the steady wind running along the river channel. This chefiti was made of cloth, evidently designed to be reused often. Gorrenn noticed that its cross stays were thin rods of metal, not wooden sticks like the toys of his youth. The tail of the chefiti was shorter than on chefitis he had learned to build. Where knots of rag fabric would have stepped the tail of a child's chefiti, a knotted rope and long brightly colored end cord adorned the bottom of this evidently nautical variant.

Orders and calls of every sort began to sound all around them. The horses were all expertly guided up low, sloping ramps. The ramps were wider than expected to give reassurance to animals not accustomed to ship boarding. The crane swung round and dock hands rigged lines at precise lifting points, the way they had done many times before. Guide wheels and tackles squeaked, squealed and groaned. The counterweights began to drop lower and lower. One after the other, the wagons rose upward, swung out over the rails of the boat, rope lines trailing behind. Each landed lightly on the deck, and were lashed down securely.

Gorrenn, and the others in their group, finally boarded the riverboat 'Dragon.' They were guided to a small salon cabin on the main deck of the boat, lined with seats. Windows provided a limited view of the outside, for those who cared to watch. River crossings were known to be wild affairs at the best of times, due to the strong currents in the Shield river. Gorrenn knew that many passengers simply folded their arms, and looked downward to fend off the effects of motion sickness. The Second Commander gave instructions quietly to everyone to not leave the salon cabin, or stare out the windows. Behavior revealing that they were uniformly not experiencing nausea might reveal their true nature to any who took note of it. Gorrenn heard a loud voice give the command "Castoff!" The boat drifted away from the dock.

From where he sat in the deck salon, Gorrenn could see the crewman who was at the bowsprit. He still held the fine cord attached to the chefiti he had launched back at the dock. Gorrenn surmised that the chefiti supplied information on the speed and direction of the wind that the pilot of the boat would need to steer the safest course. As the boat maneuvered into the current of the river, Gorrenn heard the loud voice barking out commands to set sails, and trim the rigging. In short order, the riverboat Dragon was moving down the Shield River at an alarming rate. Gorrenn had not realized that the river craft that they had boarded would be built for such speed.

The might of the Shield river exceeded Gorrenn's wildest expectations. Their embarkation point, Quolluta Jatt, is near mid-point on the Shield river. This part of the river is known to be the calmest in its entire length. Even at that, the riverboat strained and groaned at every change in direction, keeping to the calmer areas of the river channel, slowly working its way to the other side of the river. The Shield river drained the entire continent of Malitok, and showed its might at every point along its length. The passage would apparently not take very long. The boat would cross the seven passukhs of river breadth only after having traversed forty passukhs of distance downriver.

After less than an hour or so of heaving, bobbing, galloping travel, the Dragon hove over to a lagoon alongside high cliffs. The Shield river continued on past, rumbling and roaring as it went. The relative calm of the lagoon was a relief from all the movement and noise of the crossing. Gorrenn heard the booming voice again ordering sails struck, and lashed. He had not anticipated a stop along the way for any reason and asked Meddace why they had come to these cliffs.

"This is Medvazhikki Landing. Come outside, I'll show you." He led Gorrenn out onto the deck of the boat. Pointing upward, Meddace said, "Up there, that's where we're going."

Gorrenn let his eyes travel up, the hundred or so cubets of rock face before him. The boat was being docked at a pier that was lashed and bolted to the face of the cliffs. An enormous scaffolding rose upward, carrying a stairway to the top of the cliffs. Pennants on the top of the scaffolding belied strong winds blowing above. Ladders sat on either side of the stairway, providing a more direct method of ascent for the impatient or simply hardier passengers. Gorrenn could see the arms of large cranes already swung out over the dock form atop the cliffs.

As they left the deck of the boat, Massodice Parranck admonished his men to refrain from using the ladders. "We will all use the stairs." was all he said. Evidently, he didn't want any display of Warrior prowess to give away their game at this late juncture. They made for the scaffolding, and began climbing the stairway, each man trying to maintain a nominal pace on the climb.

Even before they arrived at the first landing on the stairway, one of the horses was lifted in a sling, rising past them. The look in the animal's eyes was one of fear, but under control. As they got to the second landing the empty sling sailed downward to the boat below. In this fashion, all of the horses were lifted up the cliff face, and waited for the men in a small corral next to the landing office atop the cliff. Twice during their climb, crewmen were lowered in the horse sling, preferring a rapid ride to the dock below to leg work on the stairs or ladders.

The office of the river landing at Medvazhikki, contained the other signaling point. No need for any additional height here. A signalman busied himself at the window. Gorrenn could see the signal flashes from Quolluta Jatt some forty passukhs away. Quickly orienting himself atop the scaffolding, he realized that the signal station they had left was west of where they were now. The crossing from east to west on the river had taken them around a large bend in the river that terminated here, at Medvazhikki Landing, east of where they had started.

In short order, the two wagons were lifted up the cliff face by the larger of the cranes hanging over the cliffs. No less quick and efficient than their counterparts in Quolluta Jatt, the stevedores unlashed the wagons and made them ready for the horses. The journey across the shield River had taken less than three hours.

As the horses were led to their positions in harness, Gorrenn watched the Dragon make its way across the river to a point where it would be towed back upstream by large teams of horses. For this journey, the sails would be furled and lashed, the spars and yards would all be turned to expose as small an area to the wind as possible. The chefiti, and its crewman, like all the remainder of the crew, would stay below decks. Only the pilot would be on deck to steer the ship against the awesome current of the river.

Gorrenn walked to the small corral, and began to saddle Tuzhandek for the ride over the remainder of the day. He had become adept at tying his pack in Army fashion, and getting the leg straps tensioned exactly right. Not wanting to slight his animal, he produced a carrot from his pocket and gave it to him before mounting. Dobitto's instruction had done him and his horse both well.

The time was taken for a brief supply stop at a sundry store. Szavackka had prepared a list of what was needed for the overland ride ahead of them. As they had in Quolluta Jatt, the small group of men and wagons left in an ordinary mass, again avoiding military formation. No leg straps were shown as they rode through the small town at Medvazhikki Landing. The Second Commander wanted the Warriors to be unrecognized, at least for a little while longer. Once out of sight of the town, a scout was sent ahead, and outriders posted. The small Cadre continued toward the northwest, toward Estox.

329

4

The greatest gift is to be able to give.

- The Song of Giving

The resumption of the day's journey, after the intensity of the river crossing, turned out to be a relief. Gorrenn rode his position as an outrider. He felt the tensions that had built up within him during the wild ride on the Shield River. They were subsiding, but still there. He looked within himself just enough to realize these tense feelings were the result of so much of his fate being out of his control. During the river crossing, the pilot and crew of the boat had been in control. Like the others in his party, Gorrenn had simply had to sit idly by while other men managed the situation.

The night before, in Ka'Apatta Pass, had been cold, but not as cold as it could have been. Their group had exited the pass to find a frost had settled over the plain ahead of the Quolluta Jatt crossing. The peculiarity of the winds in the pass had protected them from it. If they had not, the nights bivouac could have been very different. No one took frosts of Long Shadow lightly. If they did, they died. Gorrenn still had only his one coat and hat that he had left Daffin with. As the month of Esirren progressed, he would need heavier clothing. As their journey farther northwestward continued, he had no idea how he would get it.

Almost immediately, Gorrenn had noticed the strident intensity of the winds on the western plains of Malitok. Their path away from Medvazhikki Landing, starting as it had so high above the river, continued to rise. The western plains of Malitok were much higher than the east. Winds that blew here, often rose above much of the eastern plains, affecting weather only much farther east.

As he had grown up on the farm in Daffin, he had known the plains winds. They were nothing new to him, at all. The wind here, however, was something noticeably different. It blew steadily, coming now out of the northwest, cold. Gorrenn involuntarily drew his chin down against his chest, still keeping his gaze up, on the surrounding plain. Straightening in the saddle, every once in a while, he knew here had to be a solution for his clothing problem. What it might be escaped him.

As though he had been reading his mind, Haditthue rode up to him from his position in the center group of riders. "Cold, eh? Takes getting used to. We're in The West now. Things are different enough. You'll get a chance to learn soon."

Gorrenn bit down a shiver and said, "Learning is good, but heavier clothing is what I need right now."

Haditthue smiled broadly, "Boltenkka!" is all he said. He turned his horse, and headed back to the group.

Gorrenn knew that boltenkka were the wild bison of the western plains of Malitok. Living in the east, he had known of them only in books. Haditthue's enthusiastic retort made him think that the situation would soon change. Stories of men riding in pursuit of the enormous beasts, using bow and lance to bring them down, were the legends of his youth. He had never considered the possibility of seeing or participating in a 'zhastaam.' That was the old language name for a bison hunt.

Gorrenn started putting things together in his mind. He quickly realized that Haditthue had brought up boltenkka while he had been talking about heavier clothing. His reading had taught him that people of the western Malitokan plains wore a great amount of clothing made from the hides of the wild bison. Hats, boots jackets, pants, all could be made from the hide of a boltenkka. He had never imagined himself dressed in this manner. The prospect intrigued him. He wondered at all the steps involved in the process of bringing down such a large animal, curing the hide, and making articles of clothing from it.

The small band of Warriors made a camp for the night in the lee of small copse of trees. The break in the wind was just enough to allow for a fire to be built. The horses were fed and watered. The wagons were set on either side of the camp fire, the horses were picketed downwind from the camp, to catch a little of the warmth. So much depended on the welfare of the horses that they were always well cared for.

Szavackka made a hearty stew from the remaining food stores. Gorrenn had come to know a great many things about the larger-than-life figure of the erstwhile cook. He even saw the man foraging among the grasses of the plain for a little sprig of flavoring plant to add spice to the otherwise bland meals. The Warriors ate in shifts, sentries fed first. As the meal ended, Massodice Parranck said they would hunt boltenkka tomorrow, for food and for the hide. The sentries were posted, and the relief schedule set.

Night in Esirren on the western plain came cold. Gorrenn tried to read by the light of the campfire, but the wind would not cooperate. After a short period of trying to

335

read, Gorrenn put his book away and simply gazed at the stars. He spent longer than he would have guessed thinking about the challenges that lay ahead of him. With what Massodice Parranck had already told him, his new existence was going to be one challenge after another. His mind wandered onto the subject of the boltenkka hunt. He fell asleep imagining himself astride Tuzhandek, riding in the hunt.

Gorrenn was roused after midnight. His sentry shift would last until daybreak. The temperature had continued to fall, and his sleep had only come in short fitful bouts. Still, it felt good to have gotten some rest. Taking brief stock of himself as he took his post, he decided that it had been enough sleep, for him at least. The night sky, coming to morning, was a sight he had seldom seen. Here, in the west, the graying of the black night revealed a cloudless sky. This was a welcome omen for the new day.

5

Receive by giving.

- The Song of Giving

The small camp came to life before the morning sun had crested the horizon. Szavackka began to stoke a fire, and boil some kaffe. The fire seemed to be a lot larger than it needed to be, just to heat the kaffe. Gorrenn guessed that the kaffe would be all there was for breakfast, since he had seen the larger-than-life cook dispose of all the food stores in preparing last night's meal. The kaffe was distributed.

The Warriors drank their hot drinks, and began to make ready for the hunt. Their journey would be able to continue no further until suitable food had been hunted down.

Finished with the ersatz meal, Gorrenn began to saddle Tuzhandek, in preparation for participating in the hunt. He knew the rudiments of what was going to happen, but exactly what he would be doing escaped him. The Massodice approached, sitting astride his horse, leg straps firmly wound about his boots. "The strapping for a boltenkka hunt is different. Make your straps tight enough to keep you on your horse until you release them manually. There's a lot of bumping and jostling about. You don't want to come off your mount in the middle of a running herd of boltenkka." He turned away and rode to the edge of the encampment.

Weapons Master of the Western Army, Haditthue, began to distribute bows, arrows and lances to the assembled Warriors. The bows were heavy, combat bows. The arrows were likewise heavy. They were tipped with points as long as a man's hand, extremely sharp, for penetrating the thick, tough hide of the boltenkka. The lances were another matter entirely. Strictly built for throwing, they were lighter, and slenderer than lances used for fighting against the Giants. The steel tips of the lances were as long as a man's forearm, and sharp as a razor. Each warrior was issued a quiver of a dozen arrows and two lances.

Gorrenn followed the example of the other Warriors in fastening his quiver of arrows, and lances to the saddle on Tuzhandek's back. He used the knowledge that he gained from Meddace in tying his bedroll securely to his saddle. He made short work of making sure the weapons would remain in place until he needed them. The ride, and hunt today would undoubtedly determine whether he knew what he was doing. Likewise, he secured his dagger tightly to his side, as he had seen the others do. Haditthue had provided a sword for him to used today – no ceremony, here, it was a tool for the hunt only. Gorrenn strapped it securely, diagonally across his back, the hilt rising just above his left shoulder.

The Warriors began to mount their horses. The Second Commander's location at the edge of the encampment would serve as the gathering point. Mounting his horse, Gorrenn strapped his legs in as he had been instructed, tightly. Testing them as best he could, he rocked the saddle from side to side violently to see if his legs would stay put. This earned him a look-around from Tuzhandek, uncertain what was happening on his back. Gorrenn took the hint from the experienced war horse and joined the gathered Warriors at the camp's edge.

Szavackka stood before the gathered Warriors, a broad smile on his face. Gorrenn could not fathom why the man, regardless of his many skills, would be here before them.

He looked up at the mounted Warriors and began, "My brothers, I would not let you go to a hunt unprepared, and unfed." He reached into his greatcoat and produced a package. From within it, he removed several smaller bundles, and gave one to each mounted Warrior.

"This is so you would not hunt hungry." he said to the Warriors, as he handed each of them a package. The small wrapped bundle contained a sweet cake for each rider. The cakes were jammed full of nuts and berries, the dough rich from butter and oil.

Taking a bite from his, Gorrenn wondered if he would ever taste anything as sweet and good again in his life. Along with the kaffe in his gut, he felt well-fed, indeed. The satisfied smiles on the faces of his fellow riders said all it had to about their sense of well-being, knowing

341

that even in the middle of nowhere, the 'Cadre' had a cook who could produce suitable sustenance for them. Gorrenn learned that in addition to his many talents, Szavackka cared earnestly and deeply for his Warrior brothers.

Without a word, Massodice Parranck spurred his horse to ride out from the camp. The sky was clear, and as blue as it could be. The morning winds had whipped up from the south this morning, promising a slightly warmer day than usual. Gorrenn felt that if an omen was called for, warming winds could be seen as a good one. The small band of Warriors rode over the low rolling hills on the western high plain. The grasses undulated under the rising and falling wind. In the distance, small, stunted stands of trees fought to remain erect in the ever-present wind.

After a short while, Gorrenn asked Haditthue, "We go to hunt the boltenkka, how do we find them?" Without saying anything, Haditthue raised his hand, pointed ahead of the troop toward the west. His finger aimed at an area of the sky that was not as blue as the rest. At ground level, the change in color was evident: brown. Over that area – Gorrenn guessed two passukhs ahead – the sky was brown in color. Gorrenn realized that the brown was the cloud of dust raised by the herd of migrating boltenkka. As the new knowledge settled into his brain, the Warrior troop quickened their pace. Each Warrior called out 'Zhastaam!' The hunt was on.

6

A soul is given flight by giving.

- The Song of Giving

The morning winds had fallen to nearly nothing. This was a good thing, because the southern wind might carry the hunter's scent to the west inadvertently. A stampeding herd of boltenkka was an impossible target for hunting. A boltenkka could run as fast as any horse, especially one carrying a rider. Their speed was such that it took a well-coordinated attack to overcome their run before they got up to full gallop. Many hunts failed because the boltenkka galloped away. The history of hunting the wild bison of the western plains was filled with stories of hunts that failed, and hunters that returned empty-handed.

Boltenkka were known to be generally ill-tempered. Coupled with the quality of unpredictability, this added a lot of danger to the prospect of bringing down so mighty a beast. The charge of a five-hundred-stone-weight beast at full speed was unspeakably terrifying to think of, much less face. Many men had died, falling before a boltenkka that had decided to turn and face his pursuer.

The main artifice of the hunter, to avoid becoming the target of a boltenkka's charge, was to stay out of their central field of vision. The beasts were not terribly bright to begin with. They lost what little bit of higher function they had, when in a stampede. The tendency to run, at whatever was in front of them, was a defense mechanism that nature had provided them with. If the beasts in front of you were running away from danger, do likewise, and survive.

The small troop of Warriors had closed to less than a half-passukh when the Massodice signaled a halt. This close to the herd, speaking above a whisper was unthinkable., The low winds had shifted to westerly, and increased to the point where whispering was pointless. The Second Commander used military hand signals to divide the group in to two parties. The wisdom of this instantly struck Gorrenn. Two parties, hunting separately, doubled the chances of success. Further signals indicated that he wanted each party to bring down two animals.

The last signals were for Haditthue to lead one party. The Massodice signaled for Dobitto to join him and Gorrenn in the second hunting party. The first party would approach from a point two passukhs to the north and attack first. The second party would intercept the herd as it began to move away from the first hunters in earnest. Driving the beasts in a southerly direction, normal to them at this time of year, would contribute to a slower acceleration of the herd. Every factor had to be considered to ensure the success of the hunt.

Haditthue led his party off to the north. Gorrenn was unsure how they would know when to intercept the herd. He waited with Dobitto, the Massodice and the balance of the Warrior half-troop. The Second Commander held a lance aloft, denoting himself as the key member of the hunting troop. He looked at Gorrenn and signaled for him to also hold a lance.

Gorrenn knew then that he would learn many things this day. He would learn whether he could put together his learning and training to do what was expected of him. He would learn about marksmanship on horseback, and killing large beasts. If all went well, he would learn how Warriors worked together. He expected that he would learn much, much more.

For what seemed like a long time, they patiently waited for sign that the herd had been attacked from the north. The sun shone down on their small band, huddled in the shallow bowl of the surrounding low hills. The boltenkka herd was just over the rise before them, unseen. Flocks of jaeckles, birds that lived by picking over the droppings of the boltenkka, flew overhead. An occasional waft of scent carried toward them, over the hill, unmistakable for what it was: a vast number of large animals.

Gorrenn's question about when they would know that the herd had been attacked was answered in a fashion he could not have imagined. Traveling like a blast wave, the herd reaction to being attacked propagated itself, and took on a life of its own. Even on the blind side of a hill, the men could hear the lowing of the wild cattle turn to cries of fear. The sound of it actually went from north to south, as the herd reacted as one to the attack from Haditthue's troop.

The sound of the bison cries was immediately followed by the rise in the sound of the thunder of their hooves striking the earth, in a mad dash away from the source of the danger. Without a moment's hesitation, Massodice Parranck spurred his horse, and began to ride to the top of the hillock before them, the rest of the half-troop, including Gorrenn, close behind.

The half-troop divided into two groups even before getting to the crest of the small hill. Dobitto, Gorrenn, and Meddace bore on, straight ahead. The Massodice and two of the other Warriors broke off slightly to the south. The riders all let their mounts charge as fast up the hill as they could. At the top of the hillock, the riders all let the momentum they had built up give extra speed to the downhill plunge. The two trios of riders would strike the flank of the boltenkka herd simultaneously.

The angle of attack that they employed was critical. The riders swept down the hillside in an arcing attack staying alongside the herd as it began to gather speed. Two archers and a lancer was the typical grouping used in trying a herd of boltenkka. The first archer slowed the beast, the lancer brought it down. The second archer was in a trailing position covering the first two hunters from being attacked by a boltenkka that had fixed its gaze on them.

As the two parts of the half-troop rode down the last of the sloped ground, each rider assumed his position in the attack formation. Massodice Parranck trailed a Warrior two lengths ahead of him. There were two arrows in the chest of a sizable boltenkka even before Gorrenn's party had gotten within range of the herd. As Gorrenn drew his lance to a ready position, he saw the Massodice launch his lance from the corner of his eye. With no time to look away, he did not see the result of the throw.

Dobitto had selected a boltenkka with an arrow strike in one of the beasts' chest. Slightly larger than the animal attacked by Parranck's trio, it ran with the herd, gaining speed steadily. Without wasting time, the Weapons Master put another arrow in the animal's side, and another, just behind its left ear, in its neck. This caused the beast to slow. Closing the gap between himself and Dobitto, Gorrenn cocked his lance arm and hurled the weapon ferociously, aimed for the boltenkka's heart. The lance tore into the side of the boltenkka's chest, striking very nearly exactly where Gorrenn had aimed. The strike was instantly fatal, and the beast struck the earth. The herd swept away from the fallen beast, continuing its southward run, faster and faster with every hoof beat.

The Time of Long Shadows

Now was when the harder part of the hunt began. Without a moment's hesitation, or even a second glance at the fallen wild bison, the trio of hunters spurred their horses to a gallop. The boltenkka herd had nearly reached its full speed. They would soon become a mass of animals from which it would not be possible to repeatedly wound and kill a single one.

Fist-sized clods of dirt were being thrown into the air as sharp hooves dug into the earth. Pursuing the herd, the hunters were continuously pelted by these dirt clods. Visibility was beginning to drop precipitously.

Time was not on the side of the hunters. Dobitto raced ahead, quickly singling out a suitable boltenkka. One, two, three arrows pierced the animal's side. Alone on the side of the now fully stampeding herd, the wounded boltenkka came to a stop. Dobitto had been far enough ahead of the inexperienced Gorrenn and wounded the beast without a likely kill-strike imminent. As all boltenkka hunters fear, the animal caught sight of Dobitto, astride his horse, firmly holding his gaze on them.

Like lightning, the animal charged. Dobitto was momentarily caught off guard and did not turn his horse fast enough the avoid a collision between the wounded boltenkka and his mount. The pair were dumped over into the churned-up earth. The herd surged toward the fallen Warrior, surrounding him and his horse. The enraged boltenkka charged again.

Laying on its side, Dobitto's horse was a large target for the beast's aim. Head down, the boltenkka galloped fiercely at the pair, Dobitto struggled to get out from beneath his horse. As the boltenkka ranged within an arm's length of goring Dobitto's horse it was suddenly stopped in its motion.

Surprise that the expected the boltenkka's impact did not come, Dobitto peered over the toppled horse to see why they had not been struck. Standing next to the dead boltenkka was Gorrenn, lance-in-hand. The lance pierced through the body of the boltenkka, impaling it, pinning it to the ground.

Gorrenn had managed to release his straps, dismount and meet the charging boltenkka afoot. His lance strike had been mighty enough, and fast enough to instantly stop its forward motion. Standing there, Gorrenn, the fallen horse and Dobitto, and the dead boltenkka briefly became an island in a sea of stampeding wild bison.

Gorrenn drew his dagger and unsheathed his sword. The blades in Gorrenn's hands whirled with such speed that they disappeared from view. Gorrenn dashed and jumped from side to side, fore and back. A rain of blood began to fall, covering everything around. All that was to be seen was Gorrenn, amid a storm of flying ears, noses, heads and horns.

One large boltenkka fell to the right, another to the left. A lone female was dispatched so quickly with a throat slash that she stood in the gap for several moments while Gorrenn leapt again to the right to bring the whirling, slashing blades to bear on an angry bull. This animal was slain by a multi-strike, two-handed decapitation that took a total of two seconds. The throat-slashed female finally toppled over.

The last two boltenkka slain were merely unlucky beasts that had stumbled into a gap between the other corpses. Within a minute, the two horses and their riders were surrounded by dead boltenkka, their bodies shielding the hunters from the herd stampede. In addition to the boltenkka that they had intentionally killed, six more animals were now dead.

The herd eventually receded, trailing away to the south. The thunder of their massed hoofbeats falling away with them. The air began to give up the dust cloud raised by the herds mad rush. After the events of the preceding few minutes, the wind seemed to pass silently. The jaeckles overhead flew southward, squawking loudly, complaining about having to work for their food.

Dobitto had extracted himself from beneath his horse and gotten themselves to their feet. Neither seemed to be seriously hurt by their collision with the boltenkka. Tuzhandek ambled up alongside his rider, Gorrenn. Dobitto blinked away some of the dirt flung into his face during the hunt. He wiped his brow, checking his hand for blood. The only blood there was from the blood-rain that Gorrenn had raised. They were all covered in it.

After a minute, he looked at Gorrenn. "Men will not believe what you have done. You stood in the midst of a stampeding herd of boltenkka and killed them to make a defense for us."

"Do not tell them, then." Gorrenn felt that he had only done what he had to in order to save his brother Warrior.

"Men will hear of this, that is certain." Dobitto turned to tend to his horse. Gorrenn could only stand and survey the scene around him: dead boltenkka in a crude circle, blood and dirt on everything. He looked up to the hill above them. Massodice Parranck was there, seated astride his horse, his face black with anger. He began a slow ride down the hill.

The third member of their hunting party, Meddace, had seen the entire episode from outside the confines of the herd stampeding southward. He met the Massodice at the foot of the hill. He began to speak to the Second Commander gesturing wildly, evidently trying to convey some of the magnitude of what he had seen. The expression on the Massodice's face softened, then turned to one of astonishment, as Meddace told of seeing the rain of blood and animal parts.

Gorrenn led Tuzhandek out of the blood-circle, and away from the dead boltenkka. It would take some time to clean the blood and mud off the horse and his tack. Gorrenn decided that now was as good a time as any, and began. He drew a brush from his saddlebag, and began to brush Tuzhandek's coat, starting with his face. The horse acknowledged his rider's evident care for him with a little whinny and a nuzzle. Of course, this only put more bloody mud on his face, but it didn't matter.

"You took a terrible chance. It would have been easy for you to be killed in the middle of that stampede." the Massodice had ridden up behind Gorrenn while he was engrossed in cleaning his horse's face.

Turning around, facing his Commander, Gorrenn stood at attention, straight and rigid. "I only did what I had to. Dobitto was in mortal danger. It was the best solution available at the time."

"Yes, I suppose it seemed so, at the time. Let us hope such choices don't lead to your untimely death. You must remember, you are important to more people than just Dobitto, or even me." The Massodice shook his head slightly as head turned his horse to ride away. He halted and turned his horse back. "You have that much control over the frenzy, that you can leap from horseback and be instantly in it?"

Gorrenn shook his head, "No frenzy, just me. There was no steel, fire and lightning. Everything I did was of my choice and planned ahead."

Massodice Parranck sat and stared at Gorrenn for a long time. A younger man might have let his mouth fall agape, so stunned was he. The old Warrior had seen too much to lose control of himself like that. Meddace had told him that Gorrenn had demonstrated swordsmanship, and use of the lance such as he had never seen. The mere description of it was exciting to hear. Meddace was a very seasoned veteran. Many campaigns against the Giants were represented as totems on his lance. He would not have exaggerated in his report of what he had seen one bit.

The Second Commander of the Western Army began to think that he had to seriously reassess his expectations for what Gorrenn might be able to achieve. He was already well beyond any preparatory need from the little cadre that he had assembled to teach Gorrenn the ways of the Warrior. It was already all there: Strength, speed, skill, honor, intelligence, and brotherhood with his fellow Warriors. He could ride as well as the Riding Master. He has nearly bested the finest Warrior, his cousin Haditthue. Parranck began to think Gorrenn had been holding back with the Weapons Master, not wanting to embarrass him.

Gorrenn had returned to grooming his horse, Tuzhandek. The Massodice watched him for a few minutes more, then rode off to check on the progress of the other half-troop, to see how they had fared in bringing down the two animals he had instructed them to. If they in fact did have two, there would now be more than twice the number of boltenkka to dress.

Room would have to be made for all the extra boltenkka hide, and meat. How much meat was that going to be? Arrangements would have to be made. An idea came to him, something for later.

7

The act of giving is love made real.

- The Song of Giving

Smoke from the cook fire curled high into the Long Shadows sky. Black, and heavy, from tallow thrown into the fire, the smoke curled and fell. It rose again on the wind and drifted away. "Nine. Nine boltenkka. Nine." Szavackka repeated the litany over and over. The Massodice had told him to prepare for four animals. For one dresser that would be an imposing task.

Szavackka had done multiple boltenkka dressings before, but the thought of nine daunted him. As he had done with so many onerous tasks in the past, he put it out of his mind and bent to his work. Still the little litany of complaint occasionally escaped his lips.

It was against his nature and all of his experience to let meat go to waste, but he did not know what would become of the hundreds of stone-weights of meat that were going to be on hand. And hides. What was going to be done with nine boltenkka hides? Still, he cut, stripped and sliced, separating the meat from the bone and sinew.

Every hour or so, a group of four Warriors would arrive, deliver a boltenkka carcass, and ride of to retrieve another. There were now three. The one that had fed them last night was almost completely dressed. Its hide was drying in the sun, fur side down, on the high plains grass next to the fire. The meat was neatly stacked in crates that until today held weapons. The weapons were now loose, waiting to be wrapped in hides. Crating and close-packing the meat would help preserve it but not for long.

The Massodice had been tending the fire, ensuring that it stayed high enough to render the meats tossed into the pot. With only one large pot, a whole different type of food preparation came into play. The pot would periodically have to be emptied and some container for its contents found. Szavackka worked till midday, single-handedly dressing a boltenkka.

After the last of the animals were dragged to the campsite, Warriors were, in turn, pressed into duty, taking instruction from Szavackka every step of the way. With no fewer than eleven men to help, all the animals were drawn and dressed by nightfall. The most enthusiastic worker was Gorrenn. It seemed to please him greatly to help Szavackka.

No afternoon or evening meals were prepared. The men just took what meat they wanted from the pot and ate on their own. By the end of the day, most of the men were tired, and stuffed. Bones were carried to locations at least a passukh away in all four directions. Kehreken, the wolves, which were seldom seen, were always a present danger on the plains. Setting a place for them to feed was as much a matter of respect as it was one of keeping them at bay and surviving. At this point the 'zhastaam', the boltenkka hunt was complete. The night sentries were posted. The reliefs were assigned and the small Cadre slept.

In the morning, Massodice Parranck ordered one of the wagons to be loaded with as much boltenkka meat as possible. He instructed two of the Warriors to take the wagon back to Medvazhikki Landing. There, instructions were to be given to divide the meat between the occupants of the landing and Quolluta Jatt. The two Warriors were to wait until a signal to Quolluta Jatt had been sent and acknowledged. Three of the boltenkka hides were also loaded on the wagon. One was to be given to the Administrator of each town, one was to be given to the captain of the boat that had transported them across the Shield river. The Warriors were to wait in order to see that the instructions were carried out. They were to make sure that the townspeople knew that their benefactors were the Western Army. They were then to ride to catch up with the rest of the small Cadre.

The remainder of the meat, which was still too much for their group, was loaded on the other wagon. The weapons, wrapped in boltenkka hides were loaded as well. Some of the weapons were carried double on the riders' mounts because they constituted simply too much weight for the wagon. Even the smallest, lightest of the Warriors drove the wagon for the first day. Szavackka would walk alongside. The two parties started their respective journeys in opposite directions.

Gorrenn was outrider, again on the right. The morning ride was easy enough, the terrain very forgiving. This was a break for the horses pulling the wagon. As he walked along with the wagon, Szavackka would occasionally stoop to pick a small flower, herb, or weed, something he knew would add spice and flavor to meat that the Warriors were sure to grow tired of very quickly. Every time he stopped to harvest some small savory, he looked up to see Gorrenn watching him with an approving smile.

The midday respite was taken by a stream that ran cold and clear. Every water bottle, and jug were filled. The weather, and passing herds of boltenkka, often caused streams on the open plain to run rank and muddy. The journey to the west and north would take them into increasingly arid lands. Their destination, Estox, was in the center of an arid plain crossed by only a single river. That river, the Sileti, was bordered on either side by half a hundred passukhs of bone-dry land.

The Time of Long Shadows

The afternoon warmed to the extent that jackets could be opened. The warmth made the animals willing to move at a faster pace, even though they were all carrying, and pulling heavier-than-normal loads. Meddace had been assigned as the scout rider. He returned periodically throughout the afternoon to steer the group toward one path, or another more favorable to the passage of the wagon. Szavackka continued his herb gathering. Gorrenn had been watching the process all day. He thought to himself that Szavackka must have laden his coat pockets with a stone-weight of weeds already. Still the genius camp cook persisted in his collecting.

Late in the afternoon, when a suitable overnight camp location was being considered, Meddace returned with news that no one would have expected. He directed the small Cadre to a hillside that was half cut away with rocky outcroppings in the lee of the winds. As the troop began to encamp, he reported to Massodice Parranck, "I was not certain at first, but the sensation of being watched was too great. Several times in the afternoon I glimpsed heads disappearing behind hillocks in the distance, always to one side or the other. That was the tell-tale sign, never in front, always on the side."

"So, we will have company, for a little while, at least. It is early for them to be quite this far south at this time of year." The Massodice turned to the Warriors, and announced, "The Cigyahng are near."

Gorrenn had read about the nomadic people of the western plains as a boy. The colorful stories were always a welcome diversion from the humdrum of farm life. He was very happy to think that his world-wide education was going to continue. For the first time in a number of days, he went to sleep that night wondering what things he might see, if they met the Cigyahng.

8

Real wealth is revealed by giving.

- The Song of Giving

The next morning came with a brief, but intense frost. The temperature dropped through the morning dew-point very quickly. The balance of the day would be cold. The remaining days in Esirren, the second and last month of the season, were few. Tonight would be colder still. The sky overhead roiled with clouds at high altitude racing to the south. Camp activities automatically revealed a different tenor. Things that needed to be done were done quickly.

The kaffe tasted better in the crisp Long Shadow air. The boltenkka meat for breakfast was seasoned with herbs that Szavackka had collected the day before. Everyone ate a little more heartily, maybe even a bit more quickly. The cold wind seemed to have a bit more snap to it against their faces. The cold gave Gorrenn doubt about how he would personally cope with the weather. He would tough it out as best he could.

After the morning meal, the Warriors all made preparation for the day's ride. There were still at least several more days of riding along with the wagon, although it would get lighter each day with meals. Gorrenn began to saddle Tuzhandek. Massodice Parranck walked up to where he was with a boltenkka hide in his hands.

371

"You will need cover from here on. This will help."
He threw down the hide, knelt on it, drew his dagger, and
began to cut. He cut a crude rectangle that he then tapered
it at the long ends. In the center he slit a cross, and trimmed
back the triangular points left by the cut. The hide had only
been dried, not cured or even combed. It still smelled of
dead meat, the animal herd, and life in the wild. It was sure
to still be crawling with at least most of the parasitic insects
that lived on it when its original owner had still tramped
about the plains.

Parranck held out the crude garment to Gorrenn,
"Put your head through the center. There's a coil of cord in
the wagon. Cut a piece and tie it around your waist. We
will be able to get better fitting clothes soon, perhaps
sooner than I originally planned. That will be good since
Long Shadow seems to want to leave us a bit earlier than
normal."

Leaving the oblique statement about better clothes to another time, Gorrenn headed for the wagon to get some cord. Once there, he found only a coil of bright red cord, the type used for marking sword hilts and lances. A bit lost, he asked Szavackka if there was any other cord available to tie around his waist. The answer was 'No.' So, on it went, the dark brown-black of the boltenkka fur offset by the bright red of the marking cord.

As in many places where men work together, it was not possible for Gorrenn to return to his horse and resume preparing to ride without several catcalls. One or two humorous compliments were thrown his way for good measure. He took it all in stride.

The ride in the morning continued over the same easy-rolling plains grassland they had been on for the last several days. The afternoon ride was more rise than fall, a sign that hills lay ahead of them. The going here was a bit slower than in the morning, but still with earnest effort, passukh after passukh fell behind them. As the day's journey ended, the small Cadre found itself at the foot of the first true incline of their trek over the lesser mountains of the western Malitokan high plain.

The end of the following day found the troop deep in the hills, and definitely no longer on the open plain. Trees and shrubs replaced the endless grasslands. Paths and well-worn wagon tracks wove their way up and down the slopes.

Each day's meal consumption had continued to lighten the wagon. Even though it was a steady diet of the same thing at every meal, no complaints were proffered. The warriors ate, took their turns at sentry and scout. They rode by day, camped by night. Gorrenn had been sent to scout, along with another Warrior, for two consecutive afternoons. The whole journey had begun to take on an air of familiarity, and custom.

On the tenth day of their journey, the afternoon scout rode back to the small troop. He was not alone. A tall, ruddy-faced man on horseback accompanied him. The new man was dressed from head to toe in very neatly fashioned boltenkka hide clothing. At his right side hung a hide sling. The thongs of it were wound neatly on a quick-release fastener on his belt. Hung from the left side of his belt was pouch. Gorrenn guessed the pouch was shot for the sling. He also had a sword, dagger, and a light bow and quiver of arrows. Gorrenn new from his reading that this was a warrior of the nomadic people of the western Malitokan plains.

The two men rode side by side into the middle of the small Cadre formation, and greeted Massodice Parranck. From his outrider position, Gorrenn could hear the new man introduce himself as Dakettu – First Guardian of the Cigyahng.

"It has been a long time, my friend." Massoodice Parranck extended his arm in greeting. With a truly huge smile, Dakettu clasped Parranck's arm and drew him into an embrace.

The Second Commander motioned for Gorrenn to come closer and introduced him to Dakettu. "Gorrenn, of the Western Army," was all he said.

Dakettu was taken aback by the confusing introduction. Looking at Gorrenn's Boltenkka tunic, drawn at the waist with bright red cord. "This is a strange uniform. I do not know it." He grinned and clapped Gorrenn soundly on the chest with his open hand, stirring up a small cloud of hair and dust. "Welcome to my country, Gorrenn of the Western Army!"

Unable to resist, Gorrenn asked, "Where is your country? I do not know it."

Still smiling broadly, Dakettu looked first at Parranck, then at Gorrenn. "Five days ride from our ketema is where Cigyahng country is. When our ketema moves, our country moves with us. Within that distance, everything is under the protection of the Cigyahng. The animals, the birds of the sky, water, earth, all. You have been in our country for four days already, under our protection."

Until that moment, Gorrenn had not understood the commitment to a vast stewardship of the land that roamed the plains of western Malitok with the Cigyahng. He was immensely impressed. The Cigyahng were not merely surviving, or eking out an existence. Their objective, to live as nomads forever, belied a huge commitment to taking only what was necessary from the land. Ensuring that the land would be there for them as long as possible was as important as any other part of their lives.

"The Cigyahng are truly great then. To take your country with you is a great task." Gorrenn looked intently into the eyes of their new host.

The compliment worked its magic on the Cigyahng man. He threw his arms wide and embraced Gorrenn firmly. Looking him closely in the eye, he said, "My country will be a welcome place for you, Gorrenn of the Western Army. Tomorrow we will ride to the ketema of the Cigyahng."

The evening meal lasted long into the night. Much talk was shared over large plates of boltenkka meat. The Cigyahng was told how the small Cadre had come to slaughter nine boltenkka. He sat and stared at Gorrenn in disbelief for a long time. The easy comradeship of travelers in the open country obviated deception, there was no need for it. These were Warriors, men who fought and slew Giants. Dakettu knew anything was possible. Still, the hearing of it astounded him.

Dakettu took a long time thinking on the story of Gorrenn saving his comrade. Leaping from horseback and hewing a safe haven out of the living, stampeding herd of boltenkka was unimaginable. In the terse way that very independent people have of expressing themselves, he finally said, "Do not leap into any boltenkka herds in my country. The Cigyahng must still be able to eat for a long time."

The evident humor was not lost on Massodice Parranck who burst into laughter immediately. Looking from Dakettu to Parranck and back again, Gorrenn finally got the joke, made by the man of the land, Dakettu. Soon, everyone around the campfire was laughing so hard that they began to drop their plates carelessly. Few things bring people together like laughter. Soon, a flask of naccheo

appeared out of nowhere, was passed around.

9

To serve willingly is to give the precious gift of

oneself.

- The Song of Giving

The next morning came cold and bright, covered in
a thick frost. The small Cadre broke camp, and moved on
into the high hills. Dakettu and Massodice Parranck rode at
the head of the group. The scout had not been sent. That
would have been an affront to the 'protection' of the

381

Cigyahng. Once they had been greeted by Dakettu, they were his guests. No further advance scouting would be needed.

At mid-morning, another Cigyahng rider joined their group. At midday, yet another Cigyahng came into their midst. As the afternoon ride progressed, more and more of the Cigyahng joined them. The cool day wound down to its end as the troop, and their large escort party topped the last hill above the valley currently occupied by the Cigyahng encampment. Sixty men now rode together.

Stopping at the top of the hill, Massodice Parranck asked, "How many Cigyahng are there, now?" The sight before him and the rest of the troop was impressive. Expecting a small encampment of frontier dwellers, he now looked at what appeared to be a small city. Thousands of smoke trails rose into the sky. The number of canvas Cigyahng dwellings was too great to estimate. It seemed as though he entire valley floor, from hillside to hillside was occupied by some part of the Cigyahng 'town.'

"When I left to greet you, there were more than sixteen thousand of us. Esirren is a time of birth for many families. How many more now, I do not know." Dakettu smiled a bit, still being in high spirits, and making small jokes. The Second Commander of the Western Army was an old friend not only of his, but of his father as well. He was happy to be bringing such an old friend into their ketema.

The sixty riders were greeted warmly by the Cigyahng people. Trinkets and small bread loaves were given to each of the Warriors as they passed. Each of the Cigyahng riders was in turn greeted by their families, and left the small parade to join them. By the time they reached the center of the settlement, the Warriors were once again escorted by only Dakettu.

The Massodice warned Gorrenn, "Do not eat much of the bread, it is made from the plains grass, and will not sit well with you." Gorrenn took a bite of one of the small loaves. It did taste a bit of grass, but it was a good change from the steady diet of boltenkka meat that they had been on. Heeding his commander's advice, he put the rest of it away in a pocket, to eat later.

The passage through the Cigyahng 'town' had been an eye-opening experience for Gorrenn. All of the people were completely dressed in boltenkka hide clothing. A first glance at a group of children running, playing some game, had reminded Gorrenn of a group of boltenkka calves running on their hind legs. Hats, boots, coats and cloaks were all made of the ubiquitous hide material. A closer look at some of his escorts had revealed extremely detailed workmanship in the manufacture of the garments, totally unlike the rough tunic he wore. He had noticed that the women wore a variety of hide garments shorn very close to the nap of the hair. It had a definitely velvety look to it.

The clothing of the Cigyahng people was not the only impressive thing that Gorrenn saw. Everywhere he looked, the refinements of town living had been brought into the encampment. The pathway upon which they rode was broad enough to allow traffic in either direction. Lamps were located at evenly spaced intervals along it for night-time illumination. The cross paths they passed were equipped in like fashion. Even thought the paths were plainly laid out on the grassland, they were very organized, and orderly.

Each house that he passed - he had learned that they were called 'attanns' - was equipped with windows and doors. This was despite the fact that the entire dwelling itself was designed to be movable. The attanns were apparently all well-lit. The sun had set as they had entered the encampment, and lights were being lit within every visible building. The overall effect of the lighting, and the very modern nature of everything around them was amazing. Gorrenn began to suspect that the Cigyahng wanted for little, if anything, not living in a fixed location.

The small Cadre, and Dakettu at last arrived at the center of the Cigyahng "town.' The central space of the camp was occupied by a very long, tall version of the attann design. Called the 'attann uxun', it served as the location for the communal life of the people. The Warriors were led to its interior after dismounting and having their horses taken, each by a single Cigyahng, for grooming and feeding.

As they entered, they all needed to squint, just a little, the lights were very bright. The long attann had been prepared for their arrival with a long table set from end to end with foods of every description. As he proceeded up the length of the table to a seat, Gorrenn noticed that none of the food was boltenkka meat. At this, he felt immense relief. He had not wanted to complain, but he might have had to stop eating altogether for a day, in order to keep from becoming ill.

The head of the long table was occupied by a Cigyahng man who smiled and welcomed them all, bidding them to sit and eat. As the meal got under way, Gorrenn was informally introduced to Adurrosu, hetman of the Cigyahng clan. As hetman, Gorrenn knew that he commanded the clan's Guardians, as well as everything else in the community. As he looked at him, Gorrenn guessed Adurrosu's age at being similar to Parranck's, in excess of fifty years. He still seemed quite hale and strong.

Seated next to Adurrosu was a young woman. A very attractive young woman. Her name was Jhetahnne. She was the hetman's daughter, Adurrosu had introduced

387

her with such a gleam in his eye that it was easy to see that she was his pride and joy. Even though she remained seated, she was apparently tall and slender. Gorrenn tried not to stare, but was still quite impressed by her.

Jhetahnne had the ruddy coloration of the Cigyahng. She had dark hair, and large, brown eyes. Her presence at the table reminded Gorrenn of Llakani. The memory of his close friend startled him to the realization that he had not thought of her at all during the last number of weeks. He had been completely overtaken by events. His life on the farm, in Daffin, seemed like it had happened in a dream.

For the first time in as many weeks, he felt a sense of loss like the one he had felt on those first days, leaving his home village. The empty experience of being alone on the road, after being forced to leave the village he had grown up in, welled up inside him.

Gorrenn caught himself in reverie. His gaze had drifted to Jhetahnne, but he was frowning, almost scowling. At a quick glance from her, which she quickly returned to her place at the table, Gorrenn regained his composure. He was able to finish the welcoming dinner without letting his mind wander again.

The conclusion of the meal provided an opportunity for earnest discussion between Massodice Parranck, and the hetman, Adurrosu. Strong drink called Adoph`e, a unique, and unusual distillation of naccheo, was produced for drinking.

Much reference was made to the history between the Warriors, and the Cigyahng. Centuries of fighting against the Giants had led to a true kinship between the two groups. In instances too numerous to count, back over the centuries, Warriors had come to the aid of Cigyahng Guardians battling against a Giant attack. In like manner, the Guardians of the Cigyahng had come to the aid of Warriors. Each had, earnestly and wholeheartedly accepted the protection and brotherhood of the other.

In the way that the Cigyahng were a microcosm of the Malitokan population at large, trait inheritance had begun to take root in its people. Guardian families bore sons and daughters who were perfectly prepared to assume their parents' roles in serving the community. Dakettu was an eleventh generation Guardian. His was one of the oldest Guardian families.

Other groups in the community were also affected by the trait-inheritance effect. Weavers, wood-workers, metal workers, plant harvesters, seamsters, food preparers, and builders, all were multi-generationally endowed with abilities upon which each successive age group built its own heritage.

The evening's welcome came to an end with the suggestion of their hetman host, Adurrosu. The Warriors all rose and began their polite bidding of thank-you and good-night.

A last quick look at Jhetahnne reassured Gorrenn that he had been right about her height. She was just half-a-head shorter than he. It didn't escape his notice that she was shapely, in a very muscular way. She was carrying a sling, and shot pouch on her belt, as well as a dagger.

Gorrenn made sure to say a pleasant "Good night" to Jhetahnne before he left the long attann with his fellows. As he walked away, Gorrenn heard Adurrosu address his daughter as 'Jhetty.'

The Warriors were all conducted in a group, to an attann of their own. It was equipped with a stove for heat, and an ample supply of fuel for the night. Bedrolls and blankets were available for each man. The cleverly constructed, portable building even had a separate room,

suitable for the Second Commander. Being able to be

inside, out of the wind and cold for a night was a luxury.

The communal sleeping arrangements suited the

band of Warriors well. After so many days on the trail, and

sleeping on the ground, it was easy for almost all of them to

fall asleep quickly and soundly. Gorrenn spent more than a

little time thinking of 'Jhetty' before being able to sleep.

10

The poor know more of giving, for they have less.

- The Song of Giving

The following morning came with still air allowing

fog to drift down the hillsides and blanket the Cigyahng

encampment. Wisps of stove smoke drifted upward through

the dense mist and created a tenting effect visible to the

night sentries in the hills. Here and there, the early morning

food preparation involved enough heat to create lighted

393

islands of clear air in the fog. The heavy moist air clung to all who ventured out of the attanns. It coated their garments, dampening the start to the day. Walking through the grass, heavily laden with fog-dew, soon led to tiny sprays of water flying off their boot tips.

Gorrenn rose early, and dressed enough to head for the communal bath attann. The walk was short, and he needed to walk quickly, more because of his relative state of undress than discomfort. He wore only his military blouse – unbuttoned – he held his pants with his right hand, his wash kit and the rest of his clothes were in his left hand. His boots were loose on his feet without socks.

The fog made seeing ahead of him harder than he had anticipated. Still, it was with his head more down than up, where it should have been, when he walked directly into Jhetahnne. She was walking in the other direction.

Making as must haste as he had, he knocked her right off of her feet onto the grass pathway.

Stunned and embarrassed by what he had just done, Gorrenn shoved the contents of his left hand under his right arm and reached down to help Jhetahnne up off of the ground. As he did so, his blouse fell open. Without noticing that he had bared his chest to the young woman, he continued in grasping her outstretched hand and pulling her to her feet. Jhetahnne could not help but appraise Gorrenn from one end of his exposed upper torso to the other.

Realizing what had happened, Gorrenn quickly snatched his blouse closed. "I'm so sorry. Please forgive me, I wasn't watching where I was headed." His earnest apology had a pleading ring to it.

Adjusting her now soaking wet clothes, Jhetahnne said, "I'll just have to change clothes now. No real harm. I'll have to hurry before the meeting."

Gorrenn now saw that some of the dew drops now hung from her dark hair, even tinier ones decorated her eyelashes. He was momentarily lost in the sight of it, and her. He knew he had never seen a woman as beautiful as Jhetahnne. In that briefest of moments, Gorrenn knew that he wanted to know a lot more about Jhetahnne than their visit to the Cigyahng 'country' would allow.

"M-meeting?" He couldn't help stammering, he felt himself beginning to blush.

"It's First Day. Do they have First Day meeting where you come from?" Jhetahnne had, by now, apparently regained her composure entirely.

Yes, but..."

"We meet in the attann uxun, we even have a kellar. We've had a kellar for years. It's near the end of Esirren, the 'Sharing' discussion may be the last. I've always

enjoyed the 'Sharing' discussion more than the others."
Jhetahnne abruptly stopped. She realized that she was
gushing, like a little girl. Perhaps her composure wasn't as
recovered as she thought. She looked up at Gorrenn
intently, hoping for him to bail her out of her dilemma.

"I'm sorry, I knocked you down, perhaps the next
time we meet, I can prove that I'm not a big oaf." He
turned away, and headed for the bath attann again. His
closure of the conversation was his way of hiding his
intense embarrassment. It was all he could think to do. He
had not felt such attraction to anyone in his life. Even his
friend Llakani, whom he now knew he had loved without
knowing it, had not stirred the same reaction within him.

After finishing his morning ablutions, Gorrenn
returned to the attann where they had spent the night. The
bedroll he had slept upon was already neatly rolled and
packed. On top of it were clothes. The clothes were all

made from boltenkka hide, Cigyahng. There was even a heavy hide coat. His boltenkka hide tunic that he had worn entering the camp was gone.

"I made arrangements for proper cold weather clothing. The exchange of boltenkka hides and meat worked out very well. You will not have to worry about attracting wolves with your clothing, now." Massodice Parranck stood near the heating stove, taking a last opportunity to warm himself before their departure. He was dressed head to toe in hide clothing as finely tailored as any Gorrenn had seen on the Cigyahng.

"The bedroll you slept on last night has been given to you as part of the exchange. We will all have excellent Cigyahng bedrolls. A few of the extra weapons we carried tipped the balance of the exchange greatly in our favor. The foods provided for us in trade for the '*aged*' boltenkka meat have made Szavackka nearly ecstatic. It is now time to change your clothes and make ready to ride, the others are already ahead of you." The Second Commander picked up a packed bedroll at his feet, and carried it out of the room.

Gorrenn realized that his exchange in the pathway with Jhetahnne had led to more than a little daydreaming while in the bath attann. He now hurried a fast as he could to don the clothing provided for him. His exertion in hurrying was great enough to cause him to become sweaty as the hide clothing began to do its job of preventing the loss of body heat. He at last put on the boltenkka hide hat, and stuffed his other clothing in his pack.

Making sure to look carefully this time, Gorrenn bolted from the sleep attann and quick-marched to the corral. The fog had lifted slightly, and visibility was much improved. He arrived at the corral just as the Massodice was mounting his horse. He saw that the other riders were nearly ready to do likewise.

Hurrying over to Tuzhandek, Gorrenn saw that the bridle and blanket were already in place on the horse. He looked up to see Meddace on the other side of Tuzhandek. He gave a brief smiling nod, turned his horse and rode to accompany the Second Commander.

Gorrenn quickly saddled his horse, and mounted. He carried his bedroll and pack over his left shoulder. Riding out of the corral, he tossed his bedroll and pack into the wagon with the other supplies, bedrolls and packs. The wagon was just ready to roll out, Szavackka once again in place on its seat.

Gorrenn thought that if Szavackka smiled any more broadly, that his face would break. He apparently was truly pleased with the supplies he had gotten from the Cigyahng. Gorrenn rode along with the wagon to join the rest of the small cadre at the western edge of the Cigyahng encampment.

At the end of the grass pathway, the rest of the Warriors awaited the wagon. Several Cigyahng Guardians, including Dakettu were there. A departure escort seemed no more unlikely than the wonderful, warm welcome they had received the previous day. Before the group could move forward, Adurrosu, and Jhetahnne also appeared on horseback. They would also escort the departing Warriors, for a short distance at least.

The order was given, the column moved out. Even though the Warriors were escorted by their 'protectors,' the show was made to move in a military formation. The message was clear: "We will protect you as well." The deep friendship between the Warriors of the Western Army and the Cigyahng lived and breathed with the men who depended upon it. Adurrosu and Dakettu rode with Massodice Parranck.

After only a short distance, Jhetahnne appeared at Gorrenn's side as his escort. She was dressed as the other Guardians. She had all the weapons a Guardian would have, sword, dagger, bow, and sling. If there were any differences between the weapons she carried and those of the men, Gorrenn could not gauge it.

Pleased that she had come, Gorrenn gave her an appraising look and said, "I did not know you were a Guardian. There are many, many things about you and your people that I do not know."

"There are women Warriors, there are women Guardians." Jhetahnne stared straight ahead, trying to be as serious as she could while in the role of a Guardian. "My father is a Guardian, as was his father. Many generations of Guardian have been in my family. I have trained alongside many of my brother Cigyahng. I serve as 'One Day' Guardian for my people. The 'One Day' Guardians protect the camp of the Cigyahng within a day's ride of the ketema."

Gorrenn was even more impressed with Jhetahnne than he had been the previous night. He estimated that the assignment to duty close to the camp was the result of a doting father, not a limitation caused by Jhetahnne's less serious skill as a Guardian. He smiled and said, "Please, tell me more about your people. Learning is my true joy." The talk between two friends began, and filled the balance of the morning.

The ride continued on through the hills. North, and west, and north again, the trek wove its way through the countryside. At midday, the ceremonial part of the escort was to return to the camp. Jhetahnne asked of her father, Adurrosu, if she could continue with Warriors till end of day. Scowling a bit, and looking from her to Gorrenn and back, he assented. He gave instruction to return with

Dakettu, who sat astride his horse grinning throughout the entire conversation. Catching sight of Dakettu's grin only made Adurossu's scowl deepen.

A small midday meal was shared and farewells exchanged. Massodice Parranck sat a long time on his horse watching his old friend, hetman of the Cigyahng, pass into the distance. At last he gave the order to continue.

Gorrenn learned many things about the Cigyahng that afternoon. He learned more about the things that interested Jhetahnne. Most of all he learned how much he enjoyed the sound of her voice. The tone of her voice reminded him of many things from his younger years. It was hard to stay focused on what Jhetahnne was saying. The Cigyahng accent was fetching, lilting and with a different cadence. It brought him back to her words every time his mind started to wander.

Before the afternoon ride reached a point where Gorrenn knew they would have to separate, he made a point of extending an invitation. "You have told me so much about the Cigyahng. We are going to Estox, where I will formalize my status as a Warrior. Perhaps you could come and teach me more about your people. I could tell you about my life as a farmer."

Jhetahnne squinted and crinkled up her nose. "Farmer! Cows and yard fowl and pigs?"

Laughing a little, Gorrenn corrected her, "We were grain farmers. We did have yard fowl, but no pigs."

"If my father allows it, I will come!" Jhetahnne looked deeply and earnestly into Gorrenn's eyes. "There is so much that I want you to share with you."

The afternoon sun had at last fallen far enough behind the western hills that deep shadows now crept into the valleys. Dakettu rode from his position next to Massodice Parranck, and instructed Jhetahnne to join him. They would ride to an outlying Guardian camp tonight and return to the main Cigyahng encampment tomorrow.

"Good bye, Gorrenn" Jhetahnne said just before turning her horse to join Dakettu.

"Good bye, Jhetty!" Gorrenn called after her.

Surprised at the sound of her father's pet name for her, Jhetahnne turned around in her saddle and smiled broadly at Gorrenn.

Gorrenn thought it was the most beautiful thing he had ever seen.

11

A true gift betters life.

- The Song of Giving

Just as the ride into the hills occupied by the Cigyahng encampment had been more uphill than down, the journey began to have more downhill passages. The exit from Cigyahng protection would see them out of the hill country entirely, and back on the plains grasslands.

Nine days of serious riding still lay ahead of the small Cadre. The first four would still be within the Cigyahng purview. After that, they would be a small group of Warriors on the open plains, alone.

It was not necessarily a perilous thing for a small band of Warriors to be moving in open country. The problematical difference was that Army Cadres typically moved in force. As such, movement of less than the typical one hundred sixty-five men was likely to attract attention from someone.

Massodice Parranck decided that once the group was outside the protection of the Cigyahng, they would move with all alacrity. They would attempt to reduce the last five days travel to not more than four days. Being ahead of where anyone might expect you to be was a very strong defensive strategy.

Gorrenn spent as much of his off-duty time riding with either the Massodice, or alongside Szavackka in the wagon. He believed that once he was in Estox, events might accelerate beyond the point at which learning – at least learning from teachers and books – would be done as easily as it was right now.

He knew there were reasons for the rush to leave Ahngrist. He did not know what they might be. The fact that discovery in Ahngrist had so suddenly altered Massodice Parranck's plans was something that spoke volumes.

What Gorrenn learned about the way in which the Eastern Army had been reorganized and used for political gain troubled him deeply. It was distinct departure from the way he knew the world to be. It was an incorrect thing, a thing to be reckoned with. By whom and how, Gorrenn could not guess. Deep in the back of his mind, Gorrenn wondered when the effects of political change would reach Daffin.

Five days out from the Cigyahng encampment, the small Cadre passed the edge of Guardian protection with none of the ceremony they had met with on their arrival. The previous night's camp had deliberately been within the perimeter of Cigyahng lands for the express benefit of that protection. The fifth morning began with Gorrenn beside Massodice Parranck, once again to learn as much as he could when not riding outrider or scout positions.

The morning 'lesson' today, was more formal than most of the other days' talks the two shared. The Second Commander began, "There are five categories of tests that you will be presented with once we arrive in Estox, and all of the necessary affairs of our arrival have been taken care of. The areas of riding and lance combat, swordsmanship, bow, unarmed combat, and intelligence will all be put before you to prove your worth to the Warriors of the Western Army. Do not overly concern yourself. You are the son of Harccosshan. These are all areas in which you have already proven yourself to be truly capable."

Gorrenn needed to take a while to digest what he had just heard, and said nothing. The Second Commander continued, "You will be happy to know that by special order of Naejj Atallon, you are already recognized as a Fighter-in-training of the Western Army."

Gorrenn could not help but react with surprise. "How -? Is this even possible?"

"The Accord Riders exchanged correspondence between myself and Atallon. It is done. The Warriors here know you, and would accept you as a Warrior without hesitation. This is not so of the rest of the Army. The examination of your worthiness is necessary, very necessary. Merely being a Warrior is not what lies ahead for you. Much more awaits."

Gorrenn was, by now, flummoxed beyond reason. He sat astride his horse silently gaping at the elder Warrior.

With a hand that was much gentler than he would have expected, the Massodice reached across the gap between them and lifted Gorrenn's chin, closing his mouth and raising the downward tilt of his head.

"We will not ask anything of you that you cannot do. A good commander asks only of his men the possible, no matter how difficult it might be. The course of a Warrior's life is governed more by what he asks of himself, always."

The two rode silently for a short while, and Gorrenn resumed asking questions about the day-to-day operations of the Army, and how they progressed. His return to the mundane helped get his mind off of the things that the Massodice had just told him. The Second Commander recognized the diversion for what it was and accommodated. The afternoon discussion was likewise concerned only with the workings of the Army.

The first night's bivouac away from the Cigyahng lands was set with three night sentries instead of one. The business of the group's safety was taken seriously. Each man in turn was deprived of an equal number of hours of sleep, but no one particularly suffered. Compounding the forced high pace of the ride to Estox with shorter hours of rest would burden them all, but equally. The Massodice took his turn, though for a first watch. Szavackka stood guard as well as all the others.

The next day, Gorrenn found himself doing riding and lance combat drills with Dobitto. Drilling while keeping abreast of the small Cadre presented a few unique problems, but they were overcome. The two Warriors, having worn themselves well with a day's drilling, still stood their stations as night sentries. They slept more soundly, perhaps than the others, but would not under any circumstances cause hardship for one of their Warrior brothers by shirking their duty.

On each successive day, Gorrenn drilled with Haditthue in the rigors of training in use of the bow, swordsmanship, and unarmed combat. Each day ended with a glowing report back to the Massodice that Gorrenn had no detectable limitations. The Second Commander was also glad he had arranged for a distraction of suitable proportions to take Gorrenn's mind off of the future.

The tenth and last day of their journey brought the small Cadre to the edge of the prairie grasslands. The terrain continued to rise and fall gently, but the vegetation changed to scruff grasses and low bushes. The earth was dry and sandy.

The wind was more intense under these conditions, with less to slow it down. Periodic gusts of wind blew up spates of sand thrown into the faces of the Warriors. Kerchiefs were pulled up over faces, hats were pulled down. The cold air of the arid highlands proved the value of the clothing they had received from the Cigyahng. The tight seams in the well-made garments did the job of keeping the wind out.

Gorrenn had asked if there would be drilling in skills today, but was reminded that the only remaining area of concern for his readiness as a Warrior candidate was his intelligence. The Massodice Parranck allayed his fears, reassuring him that the drills he needed were already done. The completion of their forced march was at hand and all the Warriors were riding a bit more easily knowing it.

415

As the sun began to top the mountains visible in the distance the small Cadre crested a small rise and view the broad flat desert basin before them. In the center of the basin was their destination, the Warrior city of Estox.

> ***The gift of love begets strength.***
>
> ***The gift of strength begets life.***
>
> ***Life brings light into the world.***
>
> *- The Song of Giving*

End

The Time of Long Shadows

Glossary and Pronunciation Guide

Accord Council: Representatives of each Malitokan state

Adoph`e (Ah-DOH-fay): Naccheo distilled from wild grains and plains grasses

Aihvissuan (EYE-vi-swan): Mountain range in the extreme northwest of Malitok

Adjakka (AD-yaka): Captain in the Army

Adjakka Sa`Aeppao (AD-yaka SEYE-pow): Commander, Estox Water Supply

Ahdhamkh (Ah-DAHMK): First letter of the Malitokan alphabet

Amester (AH-mes-ter): Sergeant

Amester Sa`Aeppao (v.s.) Foreman, Estox water working crew
Apaesse (AH-pah-Eh-say): Desert plain where the city of Estox is located

Ayeth Myrtih (AH-yeth MER-tih): Outpost of the Western Army, originally a
                                 bivouac of the Ninth Cadre

Attann (ah-TAHN): Dwelling or building of the Cigyahng

Attann uxun (Ah-TAHN oogz-OON): Large, long building in the Cigyahng town

Aszoka (Ah-ZHO-ka): Sheriff, or lawman (collective for groups of same)

Banca (BAN-ka): Tobacco

Bixhan (Bee-ZHAHN): Side-bow, or crossbow

Boltenkka (Bol-TENG-ka): Wild bison of the western plain

Central West: Accord state in which Gorrenn lives

Ceyyok Myrtih (SAY-ok MER-tih): The never-ending cold death; execution
                                 method of the Szekkanni

The Time of Long Shadows

Chefiti (Che-FEE-tee): Kite

Chamakh (Chah-MAHK): Second letter of the Malitokan alphabet

Cigyahng (See-GYAHNG): Nomadic people of the western plains

Cubet (KYU-bet): 18 inches

Czhekko (CHAY-ko): Attack

Czhayegg (CHI-egg): First month of The Cold

Cztuk (Shtook): A line drawing of the point of the compass, showing fractional
degrees of direction

Darripont (DARE-i-pont): Malitokan North Star

Derae (Deh-RAE): A Giant nest or lair

Drezhkatta (Drezh-KAT-ah): Literally "sworn blood", ancient, ritualized oath of
revenge-taking, usually for a death or murder

Rehgyoraszhae (Ray-GYO-rah-zhae): Ancient Malitokan for 'democracy'

Estox (ES-tocks): Western Malitokan city

Gorrenn (GOR-en): "First Warrior"

Gorron Othu (GOR-on O-thoo): Narrow pass that forms the great waterfall forming
the Shield River

Ha'Aakka! (Ha~AK-kah): Warrior recognition, acknowledgment of an order

Haditthue (Ha-DITT-thoo-way): Warrior, Weapons, Master of the Army of
Western Malitok, Gorrenn's cousin

Harccoddan (HAR-co-dan): Sobriquet of Massodice Parranck: "Iron Arrow"

418

Harccofenti (HAR-co-FEN-tee): Sobriquet given to Gorrenn during training: "Little Arrow"

Harccosshan (HAR-co-shahn): Warrior, Gorrenn's true father: "Arrow in Flight"

Jaeckles (JAY-kels): Birds that follow boltenkka herds

Jimett (Jih-MET): Cat

Kaffe (KA-fay): Coffee

Katosse (Ka-TOH-see): Livery stable manager, spy

Kellar (KEL- lar): Minister, community leader in a worship hall

Ketema (KEH-te-mah): Cigyahng town

Lector: Presiding member of the Accord Council
Llea (LEE): Penninsula

Massodice (Mass-oh-DEE-chay): Second Commander

Malitokan Calendar: Year = 505 Days / 8 Months (1.38 yrs.)
Month = 63 Days / 7 weeks
Week = 9 days
Year Day not in any month
4 Seasons @2 months/126days
Long Shadow, The Cold, Natalis, Summer

Meddace (MED-ah-chay): Warrior, friend of Gorrenn

Muudeen (Moo-DEEN): mouse

Naccheo (NAH-kee-o): Alcohol
Naejj (NAH-ej): Great Commander

Nagybbaj (NOGGY-bye): Ancient Malitokan: "Big Trouble," nickname for
Delleyven, daughter of Jenssal

The Time of Long Shadows

Nyugati Tenger (Nyu-GA-tee TENG-ger): Ancient Malitokan for Estox 'Home of the Warrior.'

Orisoka (O-ri-SOH-ka): The name the Giants call themselves

Oroszihn (O-ro-zhin): Mountain lion of the Aihvissuan, and plains

Passukh (Pa-SOOK): Measurement of distance: 3.5 miles

Qerqel (Ker-KEL): Eagle

Rhakhamp (Rah-KAHMP): Twenty-third letter of the Malitokan alphabet

Roquala (Roh-KAH-la): Fortress

Sakada (Sa-KA-da): Cigyahng doctor

Skratadihm Othu (SKRAT-a-dihm O-thu): 'Mother of Waters,' headwaters of the Shield River

Stone-weight: Measurement of mass or weight: 14 pounds

Szekkanni (Zhe-KAN-ee): People of the Mountain: ethnic group that live in the Gorron mountains

Talo'Uah (TAL-o Wah): Last month of the Malitokan calendar

Tamukut Tenger (TAH-moo-koot TENG-er): 'Crown of the Warrior,' incomplete circle of mountains surrounding the Apaesse

Tersara (TER-sa-ra): Justice

Tharten (THAR-ten): Rat

Tuzhandek (Tu-ZHAN-dek): "Fire Gift" of "Gift of Fire," name of Gorrenn's horse

Vhorro (VOR-o): 'Guarding' Cadre of the Western Army, security police, spies

The Time of Long Shadows

Xunxti (ZUN-chee): Rabbit

Zhastaam (ZHA-stahm): Boltenkka hunt

parentheses.

Acknowledgements

Thanks to Marilyn Nardin for her editorial support. Thanks also to Linda Sieve, whose artwork adorns this book's cover.

Thanks, as well, to my wife, Christine, who listened to all my complaints with sympathy, lamented my setbacks and problems, right along with me, and enjoyed all the small and great victories that accompanied the creation of this work.

A good deal of gratitude is due The St. Louis Writers Guild (Missouri Writers Guild), and the St. Louis Publishers Association. Their members, staff, presenters and lecturers have given me not only the skills used in writing, but valuable insight into the processes of writing and publishing.

The Time of Long Shadows

www.ingramcontent.com/pod-product-compliance
Lightning Source LLC
Chambersburg PA
CBHW030539260626
47157CB00006B/2111